PURE DEAD MAGIC

Debi Gliori

A DELL YEARLING BOOK

35 Years of Exceptional Reading

Dell Yearling Books
Established 1966

For My Family and Other Beasts

With grateful thanks to the Scottish Arts Council
for keeping the wolf from the door
and to the beautiful west coast of Scotland
for providing the inspiration

Published by Dell Yearling
an imprint of
Random House Children's Books
a division of Random House, Inc.
1540 Broadway
New York, New York 10036

Originally published in Great Britain by Transworld Publishers Ltd. in 2001

The trademarks Yearling® and Dell® are registered in the U.S. Patent and Trademark Office and
in other countries.

Visit us on the Web! www.randomhouse.com/kids

Educators and librarians, for a variety of teaching tools,
visit us at www.randomhouse.com/teachers

ISBN: 0-440-41849-6

Reprinted by arrangement with Alfred A. Knopf, a division of Random House, Inc.

Printed in the United States of America

August 2002

10 9 8 7 6

OPM

Contents

Dramatis Personae

THE FAMILY

TITUS STREGA-BORGIA—twelve-year-old hero

PANDORA STREGA-BORGIA—ten-year-old heroine

DAMP STREGA-BORGIA—their fourteen-month-old sister

SIGNOR LUCIANO AND SIGNORA BACI STREGA-BORGIA—
parents of the above

STREGA-NONNA—great-great-great-great-great-great-
grandmother (cryogenically preserved) of Titus, Pandora, and Damp

THE GOOD HELP THAT WAS HARD TO FIND

MRS. FLORA MCLACHLAN—nanny to Titus, Pandora, and Damp

LATCH—butler

MARIE BAIN—cook

THE BEASTS

MULTITUDINA—rat, mother to multitudes, and Pandora's pet

TARANTELLA—spider with attitude

SAB, FFUP, AND KNOT—mythical Schloss dungeon beasts

TOCK—crocodile inhabitant of Schloss moat

THE GANGSTERS

DON LUCIFER DI S'EMBOWELLI BORGIA—half brother of Luciano Strega-Borgia

DON CHIMERA DI CARNE BORGIA—grandfather (deceased) of Titus, Pandora, and Damp

PRONTO—Don Lucifer's *consigliere* (adviser)

*All resemblance to persons living or dead is unintentional, but the author wishes to acknowledge a
definite similarity between herself and Tarantella.*

from
GREAT SCOTTISH HOUSES YOU CAN'T AFFORD
(June 1987)

StregaSchloss, Argyll and Bute

This property, three miles from the little Highland town of Auchenlochtermuchty (pop. 786), commands one of the finest views of the Kyles of Mhoire Ochone. Set in 500 acres of ancient forest and flanked by the wild beauty of the Bengormless mountain range, the house itself is an architectural gem.

Built c. 1400 on the Austrian model, it boasts several turrets, a moat (the drawbridge was used as firewood during the oil crisis of 1732), and a particularly fine example of a dungeon, seldom seen in properties of this kind.

It has been owned by the clan Strega-Borgia since 1645, when it was acquired in lieu of rent by Malvolio di S'Enchantedino Borgia from Campbell Caravanserus of Lochnagargoyle. Its charming and unusual name refers to the family's Italian heritage and the house's Germanic style of architecture.

(Rumor has it that the ghost of Malvolio's grandmother can still be seen in the wine cellar.)

The Ideal Candidate

From an upstairs window peered three pairs of eyes. The six eyes watched as a plump woman negotiated the moat, apparently unaware of the murderous Tock who dozed in its depths.

"That's the third one this week," observed a voice.

"Fourth, if you count the one that Tock ate for breakfast," said a second voice.

The third pair of eyes blinked. Too young to speak, their owner wondered if *this* one could change diapers and sing the right kind of lullaby to hush a witch baby to sleep.

Having spotted the sleeping crocodile as she crossed the moat, Mrs. McLachlan climbed the steps, sat heavily on a stone griffin guarding the front door, and gazed around. She rooted in a battered handbag and produced a crumpled newspaper advertisement and a pair of reading glasses. Wedging the glasses on the end of her nose, she re-read:

Energetic nanny/mother's helper urgently required for Titus (12), Pandora (10), and Damp (14 months). The ideal candidate will enjoy a spot of light housework, be well versed in plumbing and veterinary science, have some understanding of cryogenics, and know instinctively how to make french fries that are crunchy on the outside and soft in the middle. Hours and salary negotiable.

"Take deep breaths, Flora," Mrs. McLachlan commanded herself. "Relax. This is a perfectly ordinary job requiring no magical skills whatsoever. Think nanny. Think diapers. Think nursery teas, fluffy bunnies, and lullabies . . ." She refolded the advertisement and tucked it back into her bag. "You want to forget the past?" she continued. "Here is your chance to put it behind you. From the moment you step through this door, you will forget that you were ever a witch."

Above her head, the lintel was decorated with several cherubs peering through an infestation of stone bats. The ugliest of these cherubs had one eye that was not carved in stone but rendered in black plastic, and this slid open, rotated slowly, and finally fixed its lens on the woman below.

Upstairs in the observatory, Titus and Pandora examined the new nanny on the closed-circuit television screen. Damp crawled across the dusty floor, occasionally finding dead daddy longlegs and popping them into her mouth.

"Let me see," said Titus.

"I'm looking in her handbag just now, hang on, I'll move the field a bit."

"Let me *see*," said Titus.

2

"You're supposed to be watching Damp. I did for ages in the attic, it's your turn. . . . Oh gross!"

"What?"

"She's got hairy legs. . . ."

"Could you stop giving me the picture in snack-sized bites? LET ME SEE."

"She's nervous, Titus, see for yourself. Well, that's understandable."

Pandora stood up and surrendered her seat to her brother. Titus pressed keys and rolled the mouse with the ease of an expert. The screen in front of him filled with a close-up of the wannabe nanny's face.

"She's so *old*," he moaned.

"Not as old as that wrinkly on Monday. Remember? The one that called me Panettone and left lipstick kisses all over Damp?"

"Well, she was better than that scary one who went on about the importance of diet for raising children and said that if *she* got the job she'd make sure we ate Brussels sprouts and cabbage every other day."

"Nightmare Nanny," said Pandora.

"What does that make old furry-legs downstairs?" said Titus, allowing the screen saver to appear. A lurid pattern of purple bats flittering across a computer-generated landscape replaced the view of the ideal candidate downstairs.

"Come on, stinkpod," he said, picking up his baby sister and opening the door for Pandora.

"She *hasn't*, has she?" Pandora glared at Damp.

"Oh yes, you have, haven't you, horrible? Phwoarrr . . ." Titus held Damp at arm's length. "Let's go and meet Nanny, shall we?"

"Shall we dress up?" said Pandora. "Flour in the hair? Lipstick blood? Fangs?"

"I suppose so," said Titus, with little enthusiasm. "Rats too?"

"Perfect," Pandora called over her shoulder as she ran downstairs holding her nose. "Although Damp's derriere ought to be quite enough to put any nanny off."

Titus followed downstairs, breathing through his mouth. He opened the kitchen door and sighed. Interviewing prospective nannies had been fun at first—introducing them to the pregnant rat Multitudina, meeting Strega-Nonna in her deep freeze, Tock the croc, and all the other scream-inducing creatures that were part of life at StregaSchloss—but after one had watched the nannies turn pale and begin to twitch twenty times or more, the novelty and the glee began to pall. Frankly, it was boring. Nannies were boring. Frightening them was boring. And listening to them try to ingratiate themselves with the family was MEGAboring.

Titus watched as Pandora sprinkled flour in her hair in preparation for greeting the new nanny.

"Do we *have* to meet her?" Titus said, opening the fridge and gazing at the woeful lack of contents within.

"If we don't," Pandora said in the voice used for explaining large ideas to small people with even smaller IQs, "Mum might go ahead and hire her, and then we'd end up with someone as horrible as that one who said, 'Much as it pains me to admit, children occasionally need to be spanked soundly for their own good.'"

Titus slammed the fridge shut and kicked it. Hard. "I wonder if she tasted as bad as she sounded?" he said.

Pandora hauled Damp out of the compost bucket, scattered

a handful of flour over the baby's head, and smiled at her brother. "Only Tock could answer that," she said.

Upstairs the doorbell rang.

Latch Undone

With a sound that set his teeth on edge, Latch undid bolts, opened padlocks, and turned a vast key in a rusty lock. "You rang?" he said, stating the obvious.

Latch believed in wearing the classic butler's costume of white shirt, black tie, and black jacket. Admiring his reflection in the hall mirror for the seventeenth time that morning, he thought how the overall effect was ruined by the sight of his own hairy knees peeking shyly from beneath a kilt of uncertain provenance.

He scratched furiously, for his butler's kilt had been pressed into service as a dog blanket before it became the uniform of a servant. In all other respects, his job as Schloss butler was perfect, for it gave him a large salary, use of a small car, three rooms in the Schloss attic, and all in return for a pleasant manner with a door, being able to iron newspapers, balance the morning mail on a silver tray—and wear this unspeakable woolly skirt.

Scowling horribly, Latch opened the door. On the doorstep stood a woman. She was middle-aged, plump, carried a large handbag of battered plastic, and smelled of lavender.

"Good morning," she said, dragging her gaze upward from Latch's knees to meet his eyes. "I have an appointment with Mrs. Borgia."

Latch stared with a momentary lapse of manners. The woman's rolling R's sounded like the deep purr of a fireside cat and the lilt in her voice spoke of midges, peat bogs, sheep's wool ensnared in barbed wire, and the underfoot resilience of heather. Latch was briefly transported back in time to his youth and then instantly hurled back into the present.

"Are you going to keep gawking at me like a sheep or are you going to let me in, laddie?"

Latch cleared his throat, shuddered slightly, and said, "If modom would be good enough to furnish me with her name?"

"Heavens, laddie, what a pompous little person you are. My name's Flora Morag Fionn Mhairi ben McLachlan-Morangie-Fiddach. Mrs. McLachlan to youse. Now will you let me in?" And pushing past Latch, Mrs. McLachlan strode into the great hall of StregaSchloss.

The morning sun highlighted the fact that the house had been sadly neglected. Cobwebs drooped across the ceiling, the crystal chandelier didn't twinkle, and crumpled envelopes filled the empty marble fireplace. Breathing in the combined perfumes of beeswax and old dog with an undertone of log fire and full diaper, Mrs. McLachlan came to a halt at a large hall table, which was strewn with bills, letters, glossy catalogs, an assortment of leashes, ropes, and chains, and some exceedingly large dog collars.

Latch closed the front door, marched past Mrs. McLachlan, and threw open a door into the darkest and most depressing room in StregaSchloss. "The discouraging room, modom. If you'll just take a seat, I'll inform Signora *Strega*-Borgia of your arrival."

Latch bowed Mrs. McLachlan into the cramped waiting room and closed the door on her. "A McLachlan-Morangie-Fiddach!" he muttered. She'd probably brought her own kilt.

As the butler's footsteps receded down the corridor, Mrs. McLachlan peered at the only seat in the discouraging room. This was a sofa that looked about as unwelcoming as it was possible to be without barbed wire, large signs saying KEEP OFF, and packs of patrolling Dobermans. Mrs. McLachlan waited. A clock somewhere distant chimed the hour. Far away, a phone rang several times and stopped.

Mrs. McLachlan prodded a sofa cushion and sighed. Despite her recent promise to herself, this was one of those times where just one little magical tweak would make life so much easier. With a furtive glance around herself to make absolutely sure that no one could see what she was about to do, she opened her handbag. From deep inside it, she removed a small plastic case. She undid a hidden clip and a tiny screen popped up, revealing a keyboard underneath. Hastily looking over her shoulder, she pinned her tongue between her teeth to aid concentration and typed in S.P.R.I.N.G.S., pressed a key named TRASH, re-typed G.O.O.S.E.F.E.A.T.H.E.R., then pressed a key named REPLACE. She pointed the whole thing at the sofa and undid her tongue from her teeth.

There was a noise like that of someone being punched in the stomach with a vast marshmallow. A sort of *whufffff*. The sofa instantly looked like it had only just limped through three rounds with a heavyweight boxing champion. The sofa slumped, it bulged, it oozed saggily. Had it not been a sofa, it might have coughed and spat out a few broken teeth. Now it looked as if you could sit on it without it putting up a fight.

Mrs. McLachlan smiled. She replaced her case in her handbag and sat heavily on the sofa. The sofa surrendered. A clock somewhere chimed quarter past the hour.

Hiring Flora

"**H**old *still*," commanded Titus.

"I'm trying to," said Pandora, "but Damp wants to hold the lipstick. . . . No! *Damp!* Spit it *out*! Look at her, Titus, she looks like she fell from a great height and used her lips as a brake. Oh, Damp, don't dribble. . . ."

"What a disgusting baby," said Titus lovingly. "I think she's perfect for a bit of nanny-baiting, aren't you, Damp?" He stood back to admire the effect.

Damp's bottom lip quivered ominously.

"And now she's crying . . . told you she'd be perfect," Titus said, turning to grin at his mirrored reflection.

Pandora shifted Damp onto her other hip and gave the baby a half-eaten cookie. Stopped in mid-wail by the appearance of food, Damp gazed up at her big sister, then risked a look at Titus.

"You look *hideous,*" Pandora said approvingly.

Titus smirked, then hastily readjusted a set of glow-in-the-dark fangs, patted his slicked-down hair and pulled the collar of his cloak tight around his throat. "This ought to do the trick," he said.

"Exit one nanny," Pandora agreed. "Hold Small-and-Smelly till I sort out my veil." She passed the baby over and began to drape her head and shoulders in tattered muslin. Damp made a grab for Titus's fangs.

"Move over, would you?" Pandora nudged her brother. "Stop hogging the mirror."

The three children gazed at their joint reflections. From the mirror, three small vampires gazed back.

"Ready?" Titus wrapped Damp securely in his cloak and opened the kitchen door.

"*Got* you!" Pandora plucked something off the kitchen table and instantly stuffed it down the front of her dress.

"Is that what I think it is?" groaned Titus. "Oh, Pandora, you're so *gross*."

"Yup," said Pandora, gliding out of the kitchen in a swirl of muslin. "Let's hope the new nanny thinks so too."

Latch stood statue-still inside the door of the discouraging room, watching in disgust as his employer, Signora Strega-Borgia, fell under the spell of Mrs. McLachlan (*"Call me Flora, dear"*).

Signora Strega-Borgia was enchanted. At long last, here was a *normal* person. A person whose day would be full of nursery teas, changing diapers, singing lullabies, and reading stories about happy families of fluffy bunnies. Stories in which Mother Rabbit wasn't a struggling student witch, and Father Rabbit hadn't hopped out of the burrow vowing never to return. . . .

Three weeks ago, her husband, Signor Strega-Borgia, had stormed out of their family home in a temper and since then StregaSchloss had been shrouded in a veil of gloom. Despite the fact that their school was shut for the summer, the children rapidly turned mutinous, the staff grew surly, and everyone spoke only in monosyllabic grunts. Dust and cobwebs began to accumulate, giving the whole Schloss an air of neglect. It was as if a fog had descended on the house—everything was colored in shades of gray, and every day was a Monday.

Signora Strega-Borgia choked back a sob and peered hopefully at the woman in front of her. And there, now, in tweeds and sensible shoes, sat an unlikely savior. Here was Nanny McLachlan, who brought with her a blast of bracing Highland air, a gale that might sweep away dust and cobwebs, put a gleam back in the children's eyes, and paint the color back into all their lives. Or at the very least she would be able to rustle up a pan of fries that didn't cause the children to make gagging noises. . . .

The sound of labored breathing through the keyhole interrupted Signora Strega-Borgia's reverie. "Latch, could you let the children in? I think it's time they met their new nanny."

Latch opened the door with a tug, and Titus, Pandora, and Damp fell into the discouraging room, thwarted in their attempts to eavesdrop.

"Get *off* me," roared Pandora, "you're tearing my veil!"

"My fangs are *caught* in your stupid veil, let go of my cloak!"

Squashed under her warring siblings, Damp began to wail.

"Poor wee mite," said a voice, "will she come to me? There, pet, what's this all over your face, och, what a mess you're in." Mrs. McLachlan scooped Damp onto her lap, cradled her gently against her pillowy chest, and stroked her baby-fluffed head. Damp felt warm and safe. She plugged her lipstick-smeared mouth with a well-sucked thumb, burrowed deeper into that chest, and fell fast asleep.

Blast, thought Latch, she's got the job.

"I've never seen Damp ever do that before," said Signora Strega-Borgia in a reverential voice. "Thank you, Mrs. McLachlan. Now, Titus, Pandora, disentangle yourselves and meet your new nanny. This, my darlings, is Mrs. McLachlan."

"Hi," said Pandora in a tone of colossal disinterest.

"Bride of Dracula?" said Mrs. McLachlan. "It's a bonny costume, dear, but did you know you've got a baby rat dangling from your bodice?"

"For heaven's sake, Pan!" roared Signora Strega-Borgia, losing her cool. "Did you let Multitudina out with her brood again? How many times do I have to tell you that I take a very dim view of free-range rodents. . . ."

"Mum! Don't start," moaned Pandora.

"Count Dracula," interrupted Mrs. McLachlan, "you have retrieved your teeth, I trust? Your fangs are back in the fold? Will we see you for a bite to eat later on?"

"Very funny," muttered Titus, glaring at his shoes and avoiding eye contact with this intruder.

"Titus . . . ," warned his mother.

Slowly, as if he was wading through molasses wearing tennis rackets on his feet, Titus dragged himself across the carpet and extended a nail-bitten hand to shake. Mrs. McLachlan's hand felt warm and soft, a definite improvement on the clammy-fish, nervous-nanny handshakes that Titus had been forced to endure of late. He risked a quick look. Mrs.

McLachlan's eyes met his and immediately crinkled up in a many-wrinkled smile. Titus shut his eyes like a clam and inwardly vowed never to grow old. He retrieved his hand and used it to readjust his slipping fangs.

"When could you start, Mrs. McLachlan?" asked Signora Strega-Borgia.

"I already have, dear," said Mrs. McLachlan, patting the slumbering Damp.

"But your clothes? Personal effects?"

"Och, don't you worry about me, dear. I have everything I need in my bag."

Something smells decidedly fishy, thought Latch, nobody travels *that* light.

"That's it, is it?" demanded Pandora. "You're not even going to pretend to ask us if *we* like her?"

"You might have asked, you know," added Titus reproachfully. "I mean, I know we don't pay her or anything, but we do count, don't we?"

"*We're* the ones that'll have to spend all our time with her while *you* vanish off to Broomstick Craft at the Institute of Advanced Spelling or whatever," spat Pandora, fixing her mother with a look that could burn toast.

Signora Strega-Borgia groaned. Titus and Pandora had become decidedly prickly since their father had left, and though Signora Strega-Borgia was becoming accustomed to their verbal spats, she found it deeply embarrassing to engage in all-out warfare in front of strangers, even if the strangers did invite one to call them Flora. "Latch, would you show Nanny to the nursery while I have a word with the children? Do excuse us for a moment, Mrs. McLachlan."

"Call me Flora, dear."

Trailing in their mother's wake, Titus and Pandora followed her along the corridor and out into the light of the kitchen garden. Birds sang, bees droned, and a distant lawnmower stuttered, coughed, and stalled. The brightness of the sunlight made Titus screw up his eyes and scowl fiercely. She's going to tell us that Times Are Hard, thought Titus. Again. And how We All Have to Make Allowances. Again.

Pandora glared at the bald baby rat she'd unpicked from her dress. Bet your mother doesn't drag *you* out into the garden for A Word with the Children, thought Pandora, bet she just bites your ear and tells you to get on with chewing electrical cables.

"Do you have to be quite so obnoxious?" hissed Signora Strega-Borgia. When no answer came, she dug deep in her pockets and produced a pair of pruning shears. Picking on an innocent bay tree, she continued, "Every single nanny." *SNIP!* "Not a smile, not even an attempt to be civil." *SNIP!* "You've made it perfectly plain . . ." *SNIP!* ". . . that you'd rather they all just dropped dead." *SNIP!* "What's so awful about this one?" *SNIP!*

"She's . . . old?" said Titus.

"So's Strega-Nonna," said Signora Strega-Borgia, attacking the bay with renewed venom.

"But she's in the freezer and she's part of the family," said Titus, desperately trying to think of more reasons not to hire Mrs. McLachlan, "and besides, Mrs. McLachlan's *boring*. She won't know anything about computers, and she'll think magic is some kind of oven cleaner."

"Precisely," snapped Signora Strega-Borgia, waving her shears for emphasis. "The *last* thing this family needs is Nanny

Magic or Nanny Modem. What we need is an ordinary, straightforward, bedtime-at-nine and brush-your-teeth-a-hundred-times kind of nanny. And *that* is what we're about to get."

"I don't want a nanny," said Pandora in a very small voice. The baby rat squeaked. Large, salty wet things were dripping on its bald head. "I don't want you to have to go out to work. I don't want you and Dad to get divorced. I want everything to be like it was before. . . ."

Titus stared fixedly into the middle distance. Pandora had given voice to his deepest fear—she'd even *said* the D-word. His nose prickled and his vision blurred. No one had mentioned divorce before. . . . He silently willed his sister to stop. Whatever she was saying, he didn't want to hear it.

"Oh my poor Pan," said Signora Strega-Borgia drawing her daughter close and reaching for Titus's hand. "I know this is a horrible time for you both—you're missing your father dreadfully. . . ."

Pandora looked up into her mother's face. In a voice devoid of any hope whatsoever, she said, "But do *you* miss Dad?"

Titus froze. Pandora had done it again. Somehow she'd reached into his head and plucked out the very question he didn't dare think about, far less *say*. His breath turned to ice in his lungs.

Signora Strega-Borgia's face crumpled, her eyes spilling tears and her mouth turning into a downward curve of anguish. "Yes," she whispered, "every moment of every day. Every breath I take. . . ." Her self-control dissolved in a flood of tears.

Titus exhaled in relief. Pandora's eyes shone. Signora

Strega-Borgia hugged her children tight and in return four arms held her close and four hands patted her shoulders, stroked her face, and wiped away her tears. Unnoticed, the baby rat made a bolt for freedom, loudly squeaking its disapproval of bipeds that leak.

A Little Bit of Damp

Damp was impressed. This new nanny could change a mean diaper, sing a tuneful (if wobbly) lullaby, and didn't slobber at all when dishing out kisses. She'd watched Mrs. McLachlan folding diapers and undershirts and had noted with approval the new nanny's command of nursery etiquette. Teddies were stacked neatly on shelves, books were arranged in diminishing order of height, and all broken toys were placed in a basket for future repair. Damp's tummy was full, her diaper dry, and her head happily full of recently read stories. Now, Mrs. McLachlan sat in a sunlit corner of the nursery and mended socks.

Unobserved, Damp crawled purposefully toward Mrs. McLachlan's handbag. She pulled at a corner of the bag and it slowly toppled over, spilling some of its contents on the nursery floor. The baby sat back on her bottom and began to explore.

There was a book of the kind that Bigs read, no pictures, lots of pages; no, don't want that, *toss*. There was a lipstick in a cracked plastic tube; no, did lipstick earlier, don't want that, *fling*. There was a case that hummed quietly to itself. Intrigued, Damp reached out to pick it up. It felt warm as it vibrated gently in her hands. Turning it over—all the better to investigate—Damp unwittingly undid the latch. The case opened, exposing the keyboard within. Ahh. A piano thing, thought Damp, prodding the keys.

QWERTYUIOP appeared on the screen, followed by a prompt EXCUSE ME?

Damp pressed on, and produced !@£$%^&&&; unknown to her, the case responded, I DON'T *THINK* SO.

To Damp's astonishment, the background hum turned into a loud shriek. Damp dropped the case and did what any sensible baby would do under the circumstances. She threw back her head, opened her mouth, and howled.

It worked. Mrs. McLachlan responded instantly. "You poor wee thing. What's the matter, pet? Did something in Nanny's bag bite you?"

Damp flapped at the piano thing, now appearing to be having a temper tantrum on the shiny floorboards.

"Ah." Mrs. McLachlan paled. "You've met Nanny's makeup case. And my heavens, it's having hysterics. . . ." She picked up the case and pressed a key. Instantly the shrieks stopped, the lid snapped shut, and the faint humming sound resumed. "It won't harm you. Really. Let's put it away, out of sight, out of mind, shall we, and Nanny's book and her lipstick, then you can show me round your house? You lead with the crawl and I'll follow doing the breaststroke."

Damp set off, followed by Mrs. McLachlan.

Night drew in at StregaSchloss. The wood pigeons fell silent, the air grew cool, and in the kitchen garden, the snipped bay tree wept tears of sap. A trickle of wood smoke from the Schloss chimneys slowly dwindled to a thin line, etching a message of embers and ash across the night sky. Bats flittered out from their attic roost, their wings beating a leathery tattoo through the mist rolling in from the sea loch.

In the stillness of the moat, Tock ate an ornamental goldfish by way of a nightcap, belched a series of underwater bubbles, and dozed, dreaming of nannies and one-armed pirate snacks.

In the Schloss kitchen, Marie Bain, the French cook, blew her nose, examined the result in her handkerchief, and sneezed wetly into tomorrow's soup. She turned out the lights, hunched her shoulders closer to her scrawny neck, and sneaked along the passage and upstairs to her meager attic bedroom. In her stained apron she carried three cheese-and-pickle sandwiches and two cookbooks, in case sleep was slow in arriving and famine struck in the hours before dawn.

In the dungeons below the moat, lumbering shapes wheezed and scratched. Chains rattled, clanked, and were still. In the background, a steady drip of water on stone tapped out the nighttime like a subterranean clock.

In the wine cellar, a large freezer ticked and hummed. Deep within, in her bed of permafrost, Strega-Nonna dreamt of polar bears, creaking icebergs, and of the luminous shifting curtain of the aurora borealis.

Upstairs, propped up on pillows, soundly asleep in a full-length white nightgown, Mrs. McLachlan snored. She slept too deeply to hear the traffic of fat little knees and hands, padding across the nursery floor in search of comfort.

Damp had awoken to see silent fingers of mist pressed against the windows of the nursery. It was as if the sea loch had risen out of its bed and come to visit the Schloss, to peer in the windows and gaze damply at the sleepers within. She felt cold. She poked teddy after teddy through the bars of her crib and, using her activity center as a step, vaulted over the top rail and crash-landed onto the teddy mat below.

The corridor between the nursery and Signora Strega-Borgia's bedchamber was long and dark. Damp crawled by Braille, feeling her way along the carpet till she reached her destination. She paused in the doorway and removed several dustballs from her pajamas, then crawled full speed into the bedroom. With an effort, Damp hoisted herself onto her mother's bed and tunneled under the sheets to reach the sleeping mummy summit.

"Bog off, Damp," groaned Pandora. "Take your foot *out* of my nose."

Damp climbed over Pandora and poked the next sleeping body hopefully.

"Horrible baby," said Titus. "Take your diaper *off* my face."

Ignoring her siblings, Damp pried her mother's eyelids apart to check if she really was asleep. Two bloodshot eyes glared at her.

"You're hogging the quilt," complained Titus.

"I'm about to fall off the edge of the bed," whined Pandora.

"For heaven's sake!" exploded Signora Strega-Borgia. "Whose bed is this, anyway?"

Damp smiled into her mother's face and settled happily in

the middle of the bed. Her mother sighed. It was obvious that the baby thought that the bed belonged to her. Signora Strega-Borgia smoothed the quilt over Pandora's shoulder, tucked a wayward strand of hair behind Titus's ear, and curled herself around Damp's small body. Around her, the children slept, safe in her bed, just as they had done since their father had disappeared. And just as she had done for the previous twenty-one nights, Signora Strega-Borgia lay awake staring at the ceiling, tears tracking silently down her face as she wondered for the millionth time where her husband had gone.

Where on Earth?

In a gray prison cell, a long way from home, Signor Luciano Strega-Borgia, father to Pandora, Titus, and Damp, temporarily estranged husband of Signora Baci Strega-Borgia, woke up with a shriek. "AAAAAAARGH!" And then, for he had a headache of monumental nastiness, "Aaaa . . . oww . . . shhhhhhhh."

His eyes roamed around his cell, taking in his floor-level view of four stone walls, one slatted bench, one solid door with peephole and lock, rather too many ceiling-mounted lightbulbs searing his eyes, and what looked ominously like a potty within olfactory range of where he lay.

Things were not looking good, he decided, slowly getting onto all fours and then gently easing his stiff limbs onto the slatted bench. It *was* a potty.

This is a prison cell. This thing throbbing and pounding on the end of your neck is a head. Use it, Luciano. Think back, he commanded himself, what was the last thing you remember?

He'd been in a huff for some reason, stomping along the little lane that connected StregaSchloss with the main road to Auchenlochtermuchty. It was raining, he recalled, which was why . . .

He was momentarily distracted by the sight of a cockroach climbing out of the potty and pausing on the rim for a spot of grooming. To his disgust, it appeared to be smacking its tiny lips.

. . . which was why he'd been only too glad to accept a lift from the driver of the black Mercedes who'd stopped to ask for directions. The car's windows were made out of dark-tinted glass, so he'd been unaware . . .

The cockroach keeled over and, with an almost inaudible splash, fell backward into the potty.

. . . that sitting in the back of the car was a man dressed in black, gun lying casually in his lap, beckoning him inward with a full hypodermic syringe, which was promptly emptied into his arm . . .

. . . which would explain the pounding headache and brain-fuzz that made his recall of events so much more difficult. So that was how, but where was he now? And why? And who? *Who* had kidnapped him? He had the sneaking suspicion that whoever it was did not have his best interests at heart.

This opinion was further reinforced by a ghastly scream from somewhere outside Signor Strega-Borgia's cell door. "NO, NO, NO, scusi, Don Borgia, I so sorry I overcook da pasta, I never never do eet again. On my mama's grave, I swear I never turn eet into stewed knitting ever again, NOOOOOOOO. AAAARGHHHHHH. Not the sharks! NOOOO!"

And, disturbingly, another voice, a vaguely familiar voice,

"Act like a man, Ragu. Pull yourself together, it's not the sharks, stupido, it's the piranhas, haa-haa haaa."

Signor Strega-Borgia turned pale and began to shake. *Don Borgia? Don Lucifer di S'Embowelli Borgia?* The most evil, heartless, amoral being ever to walk the earth? The man whose idea of a noble deed was to help little old ladies cross the street into the path of oncoming traffic? Whose idea of entertainment was rounding up stray cats and cooking them in a microwave? Whose childhood had been spent in torturing his half brother—his half brother Luciano Strega-Borgia—who was currently sobbing his eyes out on a gray prison-cell floor and begging a drowned cockroach to exchange lives with him?

Yes. *That* Don Lucifer di S'Embowelli Borgia, and none other.

E-rats

Life goes on, as it always has. Worlds collapse, people go to war, divorce, and cause each other immense amounts of grief, but diapers still have to be changed, food cooked, and parents, no matter how unhappy, still have to go to work.

Thus it was at StregaSchloss. Mrs. McLachlan settled in, Damp fell in love with her, and Titus and Pandora had to admit grudgingly that her fries were indeed crunchy on the outside and soft in the middle.

Signora Strega-Borgia bid the children a tearful farewell and set off to complete her degree in Advanced Witchcraft, returning to StregaSchloss on weekends.

In the absence of her mother, Pandora opened Multitudina's cage door and allowed her pet rat the freedom of StregaSchloss. By default, this freedom was also granted to Multitudina's thirteen offspring.

Seizing the opportunity to unlock the secrets of his absent

father's vast computer, Titus moved the entire system out of Signor Strega-Borgia's study and into his own bedroom.

With these two seemingly unconnected actions, Titus and Pandora unwittingly set off a chain reaction of events that would prove to be catastrophic. This is how it began.

Damp had done A Bad Thing. Damp knew it was A Bad Thing because Mrs. McLachlan's mouth had shrunk to a flat tight line, and her eyes had grown cold and wee.

Minutes before, Damp had been gazing in adoration at the open disk drawer on Titus's CD-ROM. Above the disk drawer sat Titus's modem with its two buttons decorated with stick-on eyeballs. Titus had applied these from a sheet of cutout face parts, and thus it was hardly surprising that Damp put two and two together and arrived at pi r squared.

It's a *face*, thought Damp delightedly, what a *big* mouth—all the better to eat breakfast with. She crawled closer to the CD-ROM.

Hello, face, she thought, waving some bacon rinds that she'd found on the floor. Want some breakfast? She clambered onto Titus's desk, using its open drawers as steps, waving the bacon rinds like a flag. The open CD drawer gaped hungrily. Nice face, decided Damp, have some breakfast. With small baby fingers, Damp stuffed her bacon rinds, one by one, into Titus's CD-ROM.

It was thus that Mrs. McLachlan found her. "Damp! NO! Stop right NOW!" she commanded.

Uh-oh, thought Damp. She paused in her bacon-stuffing efforts and, at a loss for what to do next, popped her thumb into her mouth and simultaneously risked a quick glance at her beloved nanny. What she saw was not cheering. Instead of radiating Highland warmth and pillowy comfort, Mrs. McLachlan's whole being smacked of cold rain showers and grim mountain peaks.

Mrs. McLachlan bristled, pursed, and tsked. "Right, girly," she said, plucking Damp off Titus's desk, "you're coming where I can keep an eye on you, but first, a diaper change."

Sorry, face, thought Damp as she was hauled inelegantly bathroomward. Bye-bye, face.

The enticing reek of bacon rinds slowly congealing inside the CD-ROM turned it into an olfactory beacon, sending out a clear signal to those creatures that relied on their noses for survival. Several such creatures, thirteen to be exact, were idly chewing paper under Titus's bed when the first finger-like waft of bacon arrived. Thirteen noses twitched. The fourteenth nose snored, attached to Multitudina, rat mother to multitudes, who was catching up on some well-earned sleep while her brood amused themselves with an irreplaceable stack of pre-war *National Geographic* magazines. Thirteen noses found bacon to be a far more exciting prospect, foodwise, than paper and ink. Fifty-two pink paws stampeded for the enticements of the CD-ROM, squeaking and snapping at each other in their haste to be first at the feast.

Multitudina awoke to see the last of her children's bald tails snaking to and fro, dangling twitchily from the open drawer of the CD-ROM.

"RATS!" she squeaked, lunging after her offspring and gaining the desktop as the last millimeter of tail vanished into the gray gape of the drawer. Despite a rigorous postnatal exercise program, Multitudina had not managed to regain her skinny pre-pregnancy figure, and found herself unable to squeeze through the gap and rescue her children. Wild squeakings from within informed her that her children were quite happy, thank you very much, and didn't intend ever coming back out to eat paper with Mum. Having scoured the CD-ROM for bacon rinds and congealed fat, they'd found a way into another gray slot and were checking it out for more of the same. The thirteen squeakings grew fainter as Multitudina's brood investigated Titus's adjoining modem.

Multitudina squatted on the keyboard to have a think about what to do next, depressing several keys under her bottom as she considered the problem. Behind her, the screen sprang to life. A dialogue box appeared, saying SEND? Multitudina scratched an itch on her hindquarters, and unknown to her, depressed several keys simultaneously. MESSAGE SENT flashed briefly.

Abruptly the squeaking stopped. Multitudina stopped scratching and sniffed the air. The babies were gone. Here one minute and gone the next. What was a mother to do? She heaved a sigh of relief. Peace at last, she thought, and plenty more where they came from. She leapt off the desk, scuttled under the bed, and began chewing up the May 1935 edition in preparation for her next brood.

The Wager

"Titus, I'm in deep poo." Pandora collapsed on her brother's bed with a small wail.

Titus didn't respond, unless a grunt counted as an expression of brotherly concern.

"Listen up, Titus, I need your help."

"I'm busy," came the reply.

Pandora unfolded herself from the bed and came to stand by her brother. Titus muttered and tapped on a keyboard, seemingly oblivious to the presence of his sister.

"I can't tell where that stupid computer ends and you begin. Titus, if you don't stop and listen to me, I'm going to see if *it* likes Coke as much as you do."

Titus unglued his eyeballs from the screen and looked up. Pandora was unscrewing the cap from a vast bottle of brown fizz. He sighed.

"Ah! Eyeball contact," gloated Pandora. "Is there intelligent life on Planet Titus? Yes, there appears to be a large amoeba thing with an open hole in the middle of its head, but we are experiencing some difficulty in establishing communication."

Titus sighed again. "What *is* it?" he said.

"I've lost Multitudina."

"Big deal," said Titus, "plenty more rats where she came from."

Pandora glared at her brother. "And all her babies, Titus—all thirteen of them."

"They'll turn up," said Titus philosophically. "Floating in the soup, down the toilet, hot-wired to the back of the fridge . . ."

"Titus. I shut them in *here*. Before breakfast. And when I came back upstairs with their bacon rinds, they were gone."

"What did you do with the bacon rinds?" asked Titus irrelevantly.

"Damp probably ate them. But that's not the point, the point is—"

"The point *is*," said Titus, "that this is *my* bedroom, and *you* introduced fourteen free-range rats, several bits of dead pig, and one incontinent baby into *my* space. Without *my* permission. *That's* the point."

"Your Highness. Accept my humble apologies. Entering your Royal Bedchamber without permission is a crime punishable by death, but, sire, I can account for said bits of bacon and smelly baby—one is inside the other, and both are in the nursery—but where are Multitudina and her tribe?"

"You're toast, Pandora," said Titus. "Mum'll be back tonight and when she finds out . . ."

"Titus . . . ," groaned Pandora. *"Please . . ."*

"I don't like rats, remember? Frankly, I'm delighted that your disgusting rodent's done a runner."

"She's *not* disgusting."

"She's a foul-mouthed, yellow-fanged, smelly bit of vermin that's probably into cannibalism."

"She did *not* eat her babies, Titus. You've got to help me find them."

"If you're so brilliant, *you* find them."

"Bet I can," said Pandora.

"Bet you can't."

"How much?"

"A game of Monopoly?" said Titus with faint hope.

"*NEVER,*" yelled Pandora. "Frankly, I'd rather swim a lap across the moat than play with *you.*"

"Big words, big deal, Pandora. You're all talk and no action. Inside you're just a fluff-brained *girl*. You'd never *dare.*"

Livid with rage, Pandora forgot to engage her brain before opening her mouth. "I bet I CAN find them," she shrieked. "AND I WOULD, TOO, DARE! AND I'M NOT JUST *TALKING!*"

"No," agreed Titus, "you're shouting. And your eyes have gone all funny."

"I'm not SHOUTING," Pandora insisted. "I'll find the rat babies or I'll swim the moat. *Done*. Satisfied?"

"You're kidding," gasped Titus. "You can hardly swim, let alone fight off crocodiles."

"You're the one who needs water wings and an inner tube, Titus." Her voice wobbled dangerously. "And when I say done, I mean it."

Despite her bluster, reality was dawning. What on earth was she doing, agreeing to swim across the moat? Tock was starving.

Ravenous. Hadn't eaten a nanny for at least two weeks. "I mean it, Titus, but—"

"Ah! I knew there would be a but. No, you can't wear a suit of armor to swim in. Tock hates tinned food and, no, you may not feed Tock an elephant before you begin."

"You seem awfully confident that I won't find Multitudina's ratettes."

"You could say that," Titus said smugly. "But before you ask, I haven't touched them, harmed them, or even seen the ghastly beasts since last night. Now . . . *but* what?"

"But . . . I need a week to find them."

"Three days."

"Five days, then. Come on, Titus, play fair."

"In five days, that disgusting rat slob could produce another litter."

"Give me five days to find the missing babies, and if I don't, I'll swim the moat," said Pandora, crossing her fingers tightly.

"Deal," said Titus.

Beasts in the Basement

Damp sat tethered to her high chair, watching Mrs.
McLachlan prepare dinner. In a corner of the Schloss
kitchen, Latch ironed the current edition of the
Financial Times, and Marie Bain stuck out her tongue at her
reflection in the mirror.

"Ees no goot," she decided. "Meesuss McCacclong, I not feel
well."

"Never mind, dear," said Mrs. McLachlan vaguely. "Just give
me a hand with these chopped livers, and then you can have a
wee lie-down."

Marie Bain reluctantly dragged herself away from the mirror and came over to the table where Mrs. McLachlan stood
stirring, wrist-deep in gore, adding cubes of bloody jelly to a
vast cauldron full of wriggling pinkness. Marie Bain's eyes
widened as she beheld the contents of the cauldron.

Mrs. McLachlan smiled kindly as she scooped out a heaving
spoonful and offered it to the glassy-eyed cook.

"Now, *you're* the expert, dear," she said ingratiatingly. "I don't know if I've put enough salt in. Have a wee taste and tell me what you think?"

Marie Bain turned an unbecoming shade of green, and with a gargle like a drain coming finally unblocked, leaned over the cauldron and was copiously sick within.

Damp covered her eyes with her hands and gave a small moan. Latch rolled his eyes heavenward and pressed on, thankful that someone had at last passed comment on the merit of Mrs. McLachlan's current culinary offering. Nasty foreign muck, why didn't she stick to what she was good at, like fries? Still . . . at least *he* wouldn't have to eat it. Not now.

Mrs. McLachlan tsked and stirred in Marie Bain's contribution. "If you think so, dear," she said, utterly unflappable. "Still, myself, I would have added a teeny bit more salt. Let's see what the wee pets think, shall we?"

The nanny swept past Damp, kicked open the door to the dungeon, and disappeared downstairs, calling, "Wakey, wakey. Dinnertime. Here's Nanny with some tasty numns for the wee pets."

The dungeon was home to Knot the yeti, Sab the griffin, and Ffup the dragon, none of whom qualified even remotely for the collective title of "wee pets." For starters, they were enormous.

Ffup, not fully grown, was the size of a stretch limousine and was expected in adulthood to attain the dimensions of an average bungalow. Knot was eight feet of hulking, matted hairiness and Sab resembled a leather lion with wings. For the previous six hundred years, they had functioned admirably, if a tad erratically, as forms of guard dogs, patrolling the acres around StregaSchloss and devouring intruders. More recently, with the advent of the postal service and the consequent daily visits by postmen and other unplanned deliveries, the Strega-Borgias had decided that it might be safer to keep the beasts under some form of control. Hence the ropes, chains, and leashes on the hall table, and the need for cages in the dungeon.

They gathered in the gloom, nostrils aquiver, united in their disdain for Mrs. McLachlan's offering.

"What d'you call this slop?" roared Ffup, snorting twin bursts of fire through the bars of his cage. Sab flapped leathery wings in a menacing fashion and spat onto the dungeon floor.

Undaunted, Mrs. McLachlan unlocked the cage door and edged inside, dragging the brimming cauldron behind her. "I'll have none of that adolescent nonsense, Ffup, and as for you, Sab, didn't your mother teach you never to spit?"

A stunned silence greeted her query. Didn't she understand that she was supposed to run away screaming for help, not deliver a lecture on correct behavior? Knot shuffled forward, his matted hair clotted with the festering remains of many dribbled dinners. He dipped a paw into the cauldron and was just about to have an exploratory lick when Mrs. McLachlan grabbed both his paws, turned them palm upward, and tsked mightily. "I thought so . . . ," she said grimly. "Upstairs with you, and wash those paws properly before dinner. What d'you think you are, a wild animal?"

Knot burst into tears and shuffled blindly upstairs.

"Me too," yelled Ffup. "I haven't washed my claws for at least six hundred years." The dragon leapt after Knot, trailing little plosive puffs of smoke in his wake.

Sab folded his wings over his eyes and turned to stone.

"Not hungry, pet?" inquired Mrs. McLachlan solicitously,

ladling her stew into three metal troughs. From upstairs, an earsplitting scream shattered the subterranean calm of the dungeon. Mrs. McLachlan sighed. One of Marie Bain's many peccadilloes was her inability ever to come to terms with sharing a roof with the beasts. "Pull yourself together, dear," shouted Mrs. McLachlan. "They're more frightened of you than you are of them. . . ."

Arachnids in the Attic

*P*andora lifted the lid of the freezer and bailed out several boxes of fish sticks, a tray of profiteroles, and three half-eaten tubs of ice cream.

Strega-Nonna lay at the bottom of the freezer, her small body wrapped in twelve layers of aluminum foil, her head framed in a ghostly halo of frosty white hair.

"Nonna," whispered Pandora, "you haven't seen Multitudina around, have you?"

"There's not much of a view inside here," came the faint reply, and "Shut the lid, child, you're letting the heat in."

Heck, thought Pandora, dropping the lid on her great-great-great-great-great-great-grandmother's tomb. What now? Four and a half days left, and not a rat dropping to be found. Sighing heavily, and abandoning the fish sticks, profiteroles, and ice cream on the floor of the wine cellar, Pandora trekked up eight flights of stairs to the Schloss attic, a vast family museum of a loft space, full of dust and cobwebs, home to generations of spiders, woodworms, and roosting bats. It was stuffed to the eaves with ancestral memories of Borgias long gone: several hundred oil paintings of family members, trunkloads of love letters, death threats, and ancient shopping lists, a stableful of outgrown rocking horses, eight canary cages in varying stages of collapse, and, spanning the entire length of the attic, a teetering mountain range of magazines and books.

Pandora raised the heavy trapdoor and climbed in. Light filtered through ropes of spiderwebs, picking out what appeared to her to be an absolute rat Mecca. A million places to hide, a million things to chew, and a million ways to make sure your mistress has to do a synchronized swim with a ravenous reptile.

"Come on, Multitudina," she croaked, trying to sound enticing through a throatful of dust.

Nothing stirred.

"This is no place to raise a family," she tried, hoping to appeal to the rodent's dismaying lack of maternal instincts. Several spiders paused in their spinning, debated whether to argue with this hairless biped, and decided against it. "PLEASE COME BACK," Pandora yelled. "MY LIFE DEPENDS ON IT!"

She slumped onto a nearby trunk, sending a cloud of dust spiraling upward. From a window came the frantic buzz of a fly attempting to unglue itself from a web. Hypnotized, Pandora watched the fly grow more agitated, its wingbeats becoming an invisible blur, the pitch of its buzzing rising to the insect equivalent of a shriek. The web sagged under the weight of a monstrous spider whose abdomen was the size of a tennis ball, suspended on legs that cried out for shaving cream and a good razor. The spider wore bright pink lipstick, expertly applied round its mouthparts—a subtlety not lost on its intended victim, the pitch of whose buzzing reached an agonizing high C.

"Oh, for heaven's sake, can't you die with dignity?" snapped the spider, impatiently tweaking the web tighter.

The fly fell silent, save for the odd whimper.

"Tarantella!" cried Pandora.

"The very same," replied the spider.

"Pet lamb," said Pandora, with total disregard for species, "I haven't seen you for ages."

Tarantella grinned widely and popped a fly wing into her mouth. She crunched, swallowed, and extended a hairy leg to pat Pandora on the hand.

"So what brings you up here?" she asked, licking her lips with a small black tongue. Pandora found herself mesmerized by Tarantella's tongue as it sought out every tiny uneaten flake of wing, transferring each minute morsel into her maw and devouring it. . . .

"I've lost Multitudina and the rat babies," she said.

The spider shut her mouth with a snap. "Good riddance to bad rattish," she muttered. "And before you even think it— NOT GUILTY."

"Have you seen them, though?" persisted Pandora.

"Not up here. Not in my domain, thank you. I'd bite her if I caught sight of so much as a whisker."

"I've made a bet with Titus that I'll find them," said Pandora miserably.

"A wager?" squeaked the spider, rubbing all eight of her legs together with glee. "What's the prize?"

"Nothing much, just fourteen rats and the privilege of staying alive. . . ."

"And the forfeit?" the spider's mouth gathered into a fuchsia-pink O of horror.

"Swimming the moat," said Pandora.

"Auuuuk," squawked Tarantella, remembering several highly unpleasant encounters with water, and ever mindful of the legendary Itsy-Bitsy's watery fate.

". . . with Tock," added Pandora.

"Oh, what a tangled web . . . ," groaned Tarantella sympathetically.

"I'm in a real mess," agreed Pandora. "Any ideas where that elusive rodent could be?"

The spider fell silent, meditatively twirling a skein of silk around one leg. Her doomed dinner began to thrash from side to side in an attempt to break free, buzzing and wailing as it did so. "How am I supposed to think with that racket going on?" snapped Tarantella, unwrapping the trapped fly and stinging it into silence. "My guess would be anywhere near food. And being a disgusting rat, the older and moldier the food, the better." She paused to sip the liquid part of the fly from its carapace. "So much more civilized, we spiders, fresh food is far healthier. . . ."

Pandora watched in fascinated disgust as the spider sucked the fly dry.

"Now, where do we find rotten food?" continued Tarantella, warming to her theme between slurps. "We find it overlooked under sinks, fridges, freezers, and ovens. We find it in trash buckets, wheelie bins, and wastebaskets. However, these days we also find it in hospitals, schools, and old people's homes. . . ."

"Thanks," interrupted Pandora, desperately trying to avoid a Tarantella tirade. "Heavens, is that the time? Golly, must dash."

She backed away, waving limply as the spider continued.

"Incidentally in airplanes, prisons, and nasty foreign kitchens . . ." Tarantella ran out of locations as Pandora slid through the trapdoor. "Don't you worry," she called, waving goodbye with all eight legs. "Between us we'll find her. I've friends in high places. I'll put out some feelers. . . ."

At Home with the di S'Embowelli Borgias

Pronto, right-hand man to Don di S'Embowelli Borgia, knocked on the door of his master's study and entered, gliding inward as if on oiled wheels. The Don was bellowing down the telephone, his back to the door, unaware of Pronto's silent arrival.

"You're telling me that the New York sector is down as well?"

A tiny voice on the other end squeaked and shrilled, bleating excuses and apologies.

"I don't care what time it is there, *nobody* sleeps unless I say so—unless they want to sleep with the fishes investigating their concrete overshoes. Do I make myself clear?"

The faraway voice chittered nervously.

Pronto risked a respectful cough. "Maestro?"

The Don swung around to glare at him.

"Your half brother, Maestro."

The Don barked a hideous Latin threat into the receiver and slammed it back in its cradle. "What about him?" he spat.

"It's time. We've had him locked up for a month. He's demanding better food and a telephone to call his lawyer. We've hosed him down, given him a shave, and he's downstairs, waiting for you, Maestro."

Shackled to a bronze throne in the middle of a vast chamber in his half brother's palazzo, Luciano Strega-Borgia gazed around himself in a state of total bewilderment.

Over the years, his contact with his half brother had deteriorated: Lucifer hardly ever replied to Christmas cards or e-mails, his *omerta*-like silence giving rise to much speculation on Signor Strega-Borgia's part as to the murderous nature of his half brother's business dealings. Still . . . for a simple mafioso, Lucifer had done well for himself. Signor Strega-Borgia's first glimpse of the palazzo mirrored in a cypress-rimmed lake had filled him with amazement. A brief hobble in leg irons along marble corridors had brought him to this opulent room where he caught his reflection staring back at himself from hundreds of gilt-framed mirrors. Massive portraits of Borgias long dead lined the walls. His eye fell on an oil painting of a spectacularly ugly man with a nose of titanic breadth, a nose that reminded Luciano of the nasal appendage of an elephant. . . .

With an earsplitting crash, a far door flew open, and in strode Don Lucifer di S'Embowelli Borgia. As usual, his nostrils entered the room at least three seconds ahead of the rest of his body. Luciano stood up to greet his long-lost half brother.

His legs shook, his outstretched hand trembled, and his voice emerged as a squeak. "Lucifer, how . . . how nose to see you." He had the faintest suspicion that this was not the best thing to say.

Don Lucifer glared at Luciano. He had half a mind to feed the moron to the piranhas immediately and forget the rest of the plan. But no. There was work to be done. And done quickly. He needed to persuade this lily-livered goose of a man to sign a will favoring him, Don Lucifer, and then . . . well . . . the piranhas *were* a little peckish. . . .

Fixing his half brother with a smile devoid of any warmth whatsoever, Don Lucifer kissed him on both cheeks. "Baby brother. Little Luciano," he hissed, "I'm ssso glad we could drag you over here."

Signor Strega-Borgia began to protest.

"But," interrupted Don Lucifer, holding up his hands as if to ward off his half brother's words, "but, why, you must be ravenous. Something to eat, yes? PRONTO! Get the shark steaks on the barbecue NOW." He produced a key from his pocket and, with a twist of his wrist, freed Signor Strega-Borgia from the bronze throne. "And now," he said, cozily wrapping his arm around his half brother's trembling shoulders, "we have so much catching up to do. Your boy. Titus. The little runt, excuse me, the fine young man—why, he must be, what, ten? Eleven? Almost of an age to inherit Poppa's money; the stupid old, I mean, may he rest in peace. . . ."

"Twelve, actually," muttered Signor Strega-Borgia, "twelve years since . . ."

. . . Lucifer and Luciano last met on the night of their father's death, in the crowded bedroom where the old man lay, his heart running

down like an overwound clock. Don Chimera had called his sons to his bedside, where he was propped up on pillows, saying his farewells. Around him were the eleven Mafia dons (who, together with Don Chimera, divided and ruled the underworld), three lawyers, and an assortment of mayors, police chiefs, and politicians who had come to bid their old friend goodbye.

In the background, a nurse fluffed pillows, smoothed sheets, and made her patient as comfortable as possible. The crowded room was stifling, full of the smell of fear and imminent death. Lucifer, immune to the heat, sat by the fireside, roasting chestnuts in the embers and eagerly waiting for his father's death rattle. Then, at long last, he would become the new don, Don Lucifer di S'Embowelli Borgia, eldest son of the recently departed Don Chimera di Carne Borgia. Chestnuts had never tasted so sweet.

Lucifer happily planned his first day in power: item first, he thought, dispose of dumb half brother.

Item second, buy that Porsche he'd dreamt of ever since the words brrm brrm had crossed his lips.

Item third, computerize the gambling, drug-running, and extortion rackets that had made Don Chimera his millions.

Item fourth, bulldoze this old ruin and find a palazzo.

Item fifth, find a good plastic surgeon for his nose.

Item sixth, ask that gorgeous nurse to marry him.

Item seventh . . .

The door to his father's bedchamber burst open, revealing his sobbing half brother with a tiny baby in his arms.

"Poppa!" cried Luciano. "I came as soon as I heard. Look, Poppa—I bring you your first grandchild!"

The sea of bodies parted to allow Luciano access to his father's bed. To a man, the assembled dons, lawyers, mayors, police chiefs, and politicians shuffled, coughed, and examined their fingernails intently.

Holding out his bald infant to its grandfather, Signor Strega-Borgia said, "Poppa, look the baby has your hair!"

The old man choked, spluttered, and laughed like a blocked drain.

"Don't get him too excited, Signor," cautioned the nurse. "He's very frail."

Don Chimera reached out, took his grandchild in his hands, and tucked the baby safely in the crook of his arm.

"May I?" he wheezed.

"Please, Poppa—I'd be honored."

The old don began to carefully unwrap his grandchild. The baby stopped crying and gazed solemnly at the old man.

"Look—I stop the crying. What have we here, little one? No clues here at all, only one white layer after another, no, the last one is not white, it is caca yellow, like your uncle Lucifer's eyes, no?"

By the fireside, Lucifer ground his teeth.

The baby's deep blue eyes never blinked as Don Chimera unwrapped the diaper and gazed within.

"A boy!" he crowed. "My grandson . . . ?"

"Titus," supplied the proud father.

The baby opened a mouth innocent of teeth and bestowed upon his grandfather a smile of such infant perfection that the old don seemed to rally a little. "Signor Dombi, I have need of you."

One of the lawyers detached himself from the crowd and came to the bedside. "Maestro?"

"I wish to change my will in favor of my new grandson."

"Poppa . . . there is no need," interrupted Signor Strega-Borgia. "Don't be so morbid, we'll have you better in a week or two."

"Luciano, don't be ridiculous. In a week or two, I'll be compost. Now shut up and let me finish."

The nurse drew Signor Strega-Borgia to one side and whispered in his ear.

"He's right, you know, Signor. Don't waste time arguing with him, just say goodbye properly, he won't see the night out."

In the background, they could hear the subdued murmur of the lawyer and the old don, and the artificial silence caused by everyone in the room straining to overhear what it was they were discussing.

Lucifer sat stunned by the fireplace. This couldn't be happening to him.

That bald caca factory was going to inherit what was rightfully his? It was insufferable. Something had to be done. Don Chimera had to be stopped before the new will was written. He stood up, intending to call a halt to this nonsense.

It was at this point that two dozen forgotten roasting chestnuts exploded in a fusillade of what sounded remarkably like machine-gun fire. Instantly every man in the room dived for cover and simultaneously let rip with all the firepower at their disposal. All was chaos and screaming confusion. Windows shattered, wood splintered, and feathers flew. For a minute nothing could be seen but plaster dust, gun smoke, and duck down. As the air cleared, a figure appeared in the middle of the room, baby in arms, miraculously undamaged.

"Have you all taken leave of your senses?" it inquired in a voice hoarse with terror. "Poppa needs peace and quiet. . . ."

"He doesn't even need that, Signor," muttered the nurse, emerging from behind a medicine cart. "I'm afraid he's gone."

With impeccable timing, the infant Titus began to cry.

Twelve long years had passed, then, mused Don Lucifer, propelling his half brother toward the dining room. Twelve highly productive years of extortion, terror, and many murders. Don Chimera's millions lay in a bank vault, entrusted to the care of the lily-livered Luciano, waiting for Titus to reach the age of thirteen. Don Chimera's will had specified that Titus would come into his inheritance as soon as he became a teenager, the dying grandparent believing that wealth was wasted on the old. Don Lucifer ground his teeth at the prospect of Titus inheriting anything. However, he thought, a smile playing around his mouth . . . if Luciano, in a fit of brotherly love, was to sign all the money over to Lucifer . . . and if Titus was to meet with some regrettable accident before his thirteenth birthday . . . well, that would be just . . .

"Excellent!" roared Don Lucifer, dropping Luciano into a chair in front of the laden dining table. "What a feast for the prodigal brother, eh?"

Nil by Mouth

Mrs. McLachlan was cold. The dungeons had that kind of an effect on warm-blooded creatures, and trying to spoon-feed griffins with dribbly ladlefuls of cold stew hadn't exactly helped.

She sat at the kitchen table trying to warm up over a cup of tea, watching Latch as he ironed the day's paper in readiness for Signora Strega-Borgia's return from the Advanced Witchcraft Institute.

"Anything of note in the news, dear?" she asked.

Latch looked up from the ironing board. "I'm just doing the horoscope page if you're interested. When is your birthday, Mrs. McLachlan?"

"Next week, Latch," she answered sweetly, "my one hundredth actually. Do you think we'll have enough candles?"

"That makes you a Leo, doesn't it?" he said, undeterred by her sarcasm. "It says here, 'Beware of unwelcome guests. Swift action is required to eliminate them.'"

"The children must be going to catch head lice," muttered Mrs. McLachlan to herself.

Latch, oblivious, read on, "'A cool head will be required when all around are losing theirs' . . . how very mysterious, don't you think? Of course these horoscopes are all a load of codswallop, but sometimes there's a grain of truth in what they say."

"Will that be all, Latch?" said Mrs. McLachlan, absent-mindedly scratching her head.

"Take mine, for instance," he continued, doggedly sticking to his theme. "'Immense courage will be required to achieve your goals, but a tendency to rush in where angels fear to tread could have amusing consequences.' Well, I ask you, who wrote this garbage?" He threw down the paper, dumped the iron on the range next to a bubbling pan of Brussels sprouts, and folded the ironing board into a cupboard.

Marie Bain retrieved the paper and scanned the columns for her own horoscope. Against a backdrop of rising billows of sprout-scented steam, she resembled an apron-clad infernal ferret, her little eyes darting snakily along rows of type. Oblivious to the bubbling pans behind her, she read on.

Mrs. McLachlan jumped up in an attempt to rescue the supper. "Marie, dear, shall I drain the sprouts? They must surely be done by now."

The cook's eyes barely rose above the newspaper. Turning slowly to the crossword page and producing a tiny pencil stub from the pocket of her apron, she replied, "Another twenty-five meenots, Meesuss McCacclong, then they be verr soft, chust how the Seenyora like them."

Mrs. McLachlan rolled her eyes heavenward and collapsed back into her seat. Latch bent over her shoulder and whispered,

"Eet ess writted in the stars, under the sign of Mush, the over-cooked wegetable, that due to a planetary eclipse of the great star Sprout, and a cosmic collision between the constellation Lumpy Spud and Leathery Haddock, that tonight might be a good time for a little clandestine french frying. What say you?"

"The stars never lie, Latch," answered Mrs. McLachlan. "You peel and I'll sneak downstairs later and fry them."

Up in the observatory, Titus was scanning the skies, looking for his mother. So far he'd spotted three passenger planes, their lofty vapor trails gradually dispersing in the lilac dusk. The crescent moon shone from the still waters of the moat, its reflection curled elegantly round a water lily that was pulling its petals close against the night.

One by one, the stars became visible, linking dot by dot into recognizable constellations. Just as Titus had identified the Big Dipper, a wavering black dot appeared on the horizon.

Regular as clockwork, the water lilies stirred as Tock's knobbly snout broke the surface of the moat, and with a series of rusty honks and creaks, the crocodile welcomed his mistress home. The black dot grew into a blot and then a shape, then a vaguely identifiable silhouette and . . . "Mum!" yelled Titus.

Signora Strega-Borgia was back.

By the time Titus had skidded down the nine flights of stairs that connected the observatory to the great hall downstairs, his mother was handing her broomstick keys over to Latch.

"Stick it in the workshop, would you, Latch?" she said, peeling off her leather flying helmet and tossing her gauntlets onto the hall table. "I'll need you to have a look at it tomorrow. It's running very rough, and I nearly stalled over Edinburgh.

Sticky moment there, beastly thing started shedding twigs and coughing and spluttering over the castle, *much* to the amusement of a crowd of American tourists, and I'm sure I've caught a cold from hanging around up there, but we got here in the end. . . ."

Signora Strega-Borgia caught sight of her son and ran forward to give him a huge hug. "Dear Titus, how I've missed you," she whispered into his hair. She smelled of engine oil and perfume, the fragrance of mothers returned from far away. Titus squeezed her tight, and then, after a moment, looked up at her beloved face. Two miniature reflections of himself stared back out of his mother's green eyes. "Oh, Titus, I can't tell you—it's been *such* fun, but oh, how I've missed you all," she said, wrapping one arm round his shoulders. "Did you miss me?"

Latch coughed, and tactfully departed for broomstick-parking duty.

"Every night," said Titus truthfully. "Your bed was empty, and Mrs. McLachlan said we could come into hers, but she *snores*."

"Where are the others?" asked Signora Strega-Borgia. "I'm starving, what's for tea? D'you know, Titus, I haven't eaten a decent fry since I left here last week. I could *die* for Mrs. McLachlan's cooking."

"I think it's Marie Bain's turn tonight," said Titus as they walked entwined toward the Schloss kitchen.

"Oh dear," said Signora Strega-Borgia.

The smell that assaulted them from the open kitchen door could have been bottled and sold as an offensive weapon. Marie Bain hunched by the range, defensively stirring while Mrs. McLachlan hovered nearby trying to be tactful.

"I don't think I've heard of that, dear," she said. "Don't you feel that three-quarters of an hour is a mite too long for a wee potato?"

Marie Bain sniffed in a disapproving way and pointedly turned her back on the nanny.

"Heavens, dear, I didn't mean to criticize—I'm sure you know better than I how to boil a tattie, and what *is* that delicious fish you're cooking?"

Marie Bain brightened slightly and lifted the lid on seven leathery haddocks. "Ees smocked hiccup, the Signora's favoreet," she said, prodding the pallid fish, as if to check that she had, indeed, succeeded in murdering them.

At the kitchen door, Signora Strega-Borgia looked at her son, put her finger to her lips, and drew him back into the corridor. "Shhh. Don't say a word. Just find Pandora and Damp, and tell them it's suppertime."

"But I *hate* haddock and sprouts," moaned Titus.

"Bring your sisters and I'll see you in the dining room in ten minutes."

"I shan't eat it," warned Titus as his mother rolled up her sleeves and strode into the kitchen.

Marie Bain placed the last plateful in front of Damp. Damp took one look at what was in front of her and opened her mouth to howl.

"How *lovely*, Marie," said Signora Strega-Borgia. She unfurled her napkin and tied it under Damp's chin. "My favorite, smocked hiccup. . . ."

"And ees also bottled sprats," added the cook, helpfully identifying the pile of swamp greens attacking the hiccup.

"I'm sure we shall all dine like kings," lied Signora Strega-Borgia. "Thank you, Marie. Please don't wait up for us, we'll clear our own dishes tonight."

Marie Bain, wreathed in smiles, departed for the kitchen, leaving Mrs. McLachlan and the family to the privacy of the dining room.

"I'd rather starve than eat this," said Pandora, glaring at her plate.

"I did try, dear," said Mrs. McLachlan, "but Marie Bain is so sensitive to any criticism. . . ."

"Tell me about it," agreed Titus. "If we leave anything on our plates, she'll go into a sulk for days."

"I have a surprise for you all," announced Signora Strega-Borgia, producing a slim metal rod from beneath the table. "I learned some new spells at the Institute this week—nothing too adventurous, just Level Two Shrinking, Advanced Enlarging, and a smattering of Transformation."

"You first, Titus," she said, sliding his plate toward herself. Her wand described several circles around the plate, at first, slow and deliberate, and then as she gained confidence, faster and faster, until the tip of the wand became a blur of light. The unwanted plateful began to fade, as if all its color was being drained away, until it looked like a black-and-white line drawing of a plate with blobs of food on it. The candles in the middle of the table flickered as Signora Strega-Borgia used her wand as an eraser, and bit by bit, rubbed out the inedible dinner.

"Wow!" gasped Pandora, looking meaningfully at her brother. "I wish I could do that."

"Mum, that's really cool, but . . . ," said Titus.

"Ow!" yelled Signora Strega-Borgia, dropping the wand onto the tablecloth. "The beastly thing keeps on overheating." She plucked the wand from the smoldering tablecloth and plunged it into a nearby wine bottle, where it bubbled and spat for a moment before subsiding with a small eruption of steam. "Pretty neat, huh?" she said in triumph. "Who's next?"

"Mum." Titus clutched his stomach. "I'm *starving*."

"Ah," said Signora Strega-Borgia, decanting the wand from the wine bottle. "I'm not very adept at the next bit—we did do a spot of fizzy-water-into-claret and princes-into-frogs stuff— let's see if I can remember . . ."

Mrs. McLachlan and the family watched in amazement as Signora Strega-Borgia used her wand to draw lines of light on the tablecloth. The lines began to describe the shape of a large pudding bowl full of something. Damp's eyes grew wide. Signora Strega-Borgia's wand was behaving like a paintbrush, filling color in between the lines.

"Very nice, dear," said Mrs. McLachlan approvingly. "Lemon meringue pie and mint ice cream, by the look of it?"

A puff of smoke came from the end of the wand, and with a small wheeze, it flopped, dangling from its owner's hand like a dead eel. "Blast this thing," muttered Signora Strega-Borgia, trying to make the wand stand up straight. The wand curled up like a pretzel and gave out a dying rattle.

Meanwhile, Titus dug his spoon into his ice cream and scooped a huge spoonful into his mouth. "Blaaark," he spat. "Brussels sprout ice cream!"

Damp's bottom lip popped out and began to quiver.

Titus approached the pie with extreme caution, dissecting a minute sliver and gingerly placing it on his tongue.

"Well?" asked Pandora, enjoying the delightful spectacle of her brother gagging into his napkin. "Do tell?"

Titus grabbed his water glass and rinsed his mouth thoroughly. "Haddock and potato meringue pie," he groaned.

Mrs. McLachlan rose to her feet, piled up the unwanted plates, and scraped the leftovers into an ornamental potpourri bowl.

"How are you going to hide that lot from Marie Bain?" asked Pandora.

Mrs. McLachlan poked her head round the door to the hall and called, "Kno-ot . . . Ffu-u-up . . . Sab . . . Din-dins!"

The approaching thunder of yeti pad, dragon claw, and griffin toe was punctuated by a crash and a crescendo of shrieks from Marie Bain.

"Coast's clear," announced Mrs. McLachlan, heading out the door with the bowl of leftovers. "Anyone for fries?"

The Night Outside . . .

Signora Strega-Borgia was walking the pets before bedtime. Tock waddled happily alongside his beloved mistress, Ffup and Sab flew overhead, and Knot lagged behind, occasionally rolling in dirt and sniffing in puddles.

Signora Strega-Borgia swung their leashes and inhaled the night air. "Just a bit farther," she said, "and then we must go home to our beds. . . . Sab and Ffup, you haven't gone yet, have you?"

Two spectacular crashes in the bushes, followed by a spreading smell, informed her that the griffin and the dragon had performed obediently.

"Good boys," she said encouragingly. "But, oh dear, those dinner leftovers didn't agree with you, did they?"

Knot belched loudly from behind a flowering shrub. Its white flowers wilted slightly, and Tock stopped in his tracks, covered his nose with his claws, and honked piteously.

In the distance, an owl hooted. Knot listened intently and began to drool. "Not now, Knot. You've *been* fed," said Signora Strega-Borgia, stopping by the edge of the duck pond to shake a stone free of her shoe.

Tock sighed. It had been a few weeks since he'd sunk his teeth into a decent nanny, and although it was too dark to see the ducks, he could *smell* them. He opened his jaws with a creak and dipped an experimental claw into the water. . . . Signora Strega-Borgia sneezed explosively. At once, five startled ducks took flight and a lovelorn toad fell backward off his lily pad and sank into the darkness of the pond. Tock closed his jaws with a disappointed honk.

"Blast it," said Signora Strega-Borgia, sneezing again. Tock gazed at his mistress in alarm as she rooted around in her pockets, hunting for something to wipe her nose with.

"Aaaachoo! Not *again*. Oh, where are my tissues? Aaaachoo! Oh *dear* . . . Knot? Knot, come here, pet."

The yeti obediently shuffled closer until he stood beside Signora Strega-Borgia. She took one of his matted and hairy arms, brought it up to her face, and delicately wiped her nose with it.

"Better. Thanks, Knot, but stay close till we're home, I might need you again. Aaachoo!" Sneezing fitfully, Signora Strega-Borgia headed for home. The StregaSchloss lay before her, tucked snugly into a fold of land that tapered off into the sea loch. Faraway lights glimmered across the water. The distant puttering of a lobster boat putting out to sea and the leathery flap of Sab and Ffup wheeling around overhead were the only sounds disturbing the silence. StregaSchloss looked like a ship at sea.

Unfortunately, a captainless ship, thought Signora Strega-Borgia, blinking rapidly to forestall the inevitable tears that came when her thoughts turned to her missing husband. Captainless, but not adrift, she reminded herself. Sailing with Mrs. McLachlan firmly at the helm. For the umpteenth time, Signora Strega-Borgia gave silent thanks for the good fortune that had brought dear, sensible Nanny McLachlan to StregaSchloss.

Her home beckoned, its dark mass dotted here and there with lights shining from windows, magically afloat in a night garden.

"Aaachoo!" sneezed Signora Strega-Borgia, breaking the spell.

Wordlessly, Knot extended an arm.

...And the Night Within

I'm only doing this because I'm desperate, thought Pandora, tiptoeing into her mother's bedroom. The room was in darkness, but she could just about make out the shape of Signora Strega-Borgia's briefcase on top of her bed. I wouldn't do this normally, you understand, continued Pandora, undoing the buckles and pressing open the latch. Raising the lid, she opened the briefcase and gazed inside.

On first glance, the contents were disappointing. Ordinary, even. One half-eaten chicken sandwich plus crumpled cookie wrapper, one pocket calculator, a small cell phone, a packet of assorted wands (with seven left in the pack), and one two-ring binder. What, no toads? thought Pandora. No vials and potions? Not even a Collapsa Cauldron or some dehydrated Eye of Newt? She picked out the packet of disposable wands and put three in her pajama pocket. In the darkness, she failed to notice the small print on one wand that proclaimed it to be a *Contrawand—reverses spells, undoes charms, and nixes hexes,* and in even smaller print: *The manufacturers recommend six (6) uses only before safe disposal as hazardous magical waste.*

Intrigued by the two-ring binder, Pandora found it to be full of page upon page of her mother's handwriting. Hmm, thought Pandora, this looks promising. . . . She meditatively ate the remainder of the chicken sandwich, reading by the dim light from the open doorway, and after a couple of pages, found what she was looking for. It read:

WK 4 Transthingummy, Shrinking, and ~~Eggsdgeration~~ ~~Exxageration~~ Exaggerashun
Experiment One — water into wine,
princes into frogs, etc.
<u>Wand</u>   ⊚ ×7   ⊚ ×9   ⤳⤷ ×1   ⊚ ×3   ↑
                                                !

n.b. steady hand required

Downstairs, the front door opened and Pandora heard her mother's voice calling the pets to order. A honk and a splash from the moat signified Tock's bedtime and the sound of footsteps and rattling chains meant that Signora Strega-Borgia was leading Sab, Ffup, and Knot back to the dungeon. That gave Pandora about two minutes to leave the bedroom exactly as she had found it.

Stuffing everything back into the briefcase, she carefully removed three relevant pages of spells from the two-ring binder, wedged them under her pajama top, and replaced the binder in the briefcase. She had just enough time to press the latch closed, buckle the straps, and hurl the briefcase back on the bed before she heard her mother sneezing her way back up from the dungeon.

Pandora slipped away along the corridor and up one flight of steps to her own bedroom. Judging by the lack of light from under Titus's door, he had fallen asleep, happy in the knowledge that his sister was one day closer to her swim with Tock. "Just you wait, Titus," she muttered, pulling the quilt over her head and turning on her flashlight. "First I'll get to grips with these wands, and then . . . you're toast." She removed the sheets of spells from under her pajama top and began to commit them to memory.

The Schloss slept, the heavy air full of dreams, the gentle lapping of waves on the shore forming a tidal rhythm to doze by. Deep in her polar night, Strega-Nonna dreamt of igloos and ice. Her freezer bed hummed and clicked, powered by a thin cable that snaked between the sleeper and the wall socket. The cable trailed across several yards of floor, dipping for half its length into a yellow puddle. This puddle consisted of fluids that had oozed out from Pandora's neglected pile of fish sticks, profiteroles, and ice cream. At first it was a rather nasty combination of fish drip, chocolate and cream leak, and banana, mint-chocolate-chip, and strawberry ooze. That had been fourteen hours ago.

In the gentle warmth of the cellar, the puddle now could be safely described as a biological hazard. Bacteria formed, grew, reached adulthood, had babies, and became grandparents. Teeming millions fed on the puddle, came back for second helpings, belched microscopically, and, due to the richness of the feast, passed large quantities of noxious gases. The puddle bubbled and heaved like a small swamp. The puddle stank. To Multitudina, who had missed bacon rind breakfast, the puddle was the nearest thing to heaven that she'd ever smelled.

Oh YES, she thought, running at it at full tilt. Oh YES, oh YES, she continued, rolling up her top lip to expose her long yellow teeth. Mmmhmmm, sweet fishy rancidness, mmhmm, sour cheesy putrefaction, mmHMMM, taste that decay, mmHmMM? Rubbery chewiness? . . . BANG! Uh-oh . . . FLASSSSH.

Those fireworks were quite unnecessary, thought Multitudina, rubbing her burnt nose and assessing herself for whisker loss. Good food doesn't need that kind of embellishment. Squeaking with outrage, she bolted out of the cellar and scuttled upstairs to her refuge under Titus's bed.

The freezer, in the silent way of such things, began to adapt to life as a large box. The thaw had begun.

Magic for Beginners

Morning dawned, wet and gray at StregaSchloss. Rain pitted the surface of the moat like a bad case of acne, and Tock sulked under a water lily thicket. Puddles formed, gutters ran, and windows misted up inside. The dungeons tended to seep and drip in bad weather, and out of pity, Mrs. McLachlan had allowed Sab, Ffup, and Knot into the kitchen to dry off. By the range, Marie Bain was stirring a pot of volcanic porridge, her yellow feet incongruously clad in fluffy pink slippers adorned with little bunnies. Mouth pursed and eyes grimly slitted, she was trying to ignore Knot, who gazed fixedly at the cook's feet and hoped against hope that she was wearing his breakfast.

Titus sat opposite the beasts, sneezing occasionally and steadily working his way through the healthy part of breakfast in the hope of reaching the unhealthy part before his jaws collapsed from exhaustion.

"More muesli, dear?"

"Nnnng," he replied, chewing heroically.

When Mrs. McLachlan turned her back on him to assess the status of her baking raspberry muffins, Titus slid his muesli bowl over to Ffup.

The dragon glared at him. "Forget it, pal," he hissed, pushing it back to Titus with a disdainful talon. "After last night's offering, I'm *never* going to eat your leftovers again."

Titus raised a hopeful eyebrow at Sab. The griffin's eyeballs immediately turned to stone. Titus sighed. Knot was oblivious to everything but Marie Bain's feet, encased as they were in such delicious pink fluffiness. . . . With another deep sigh, Titus began his fortieth spoonful of muesli.

Upstairs, Pandora was examining the plunder from her mother's briefcase.

"With this kind of spell, I could shrink you as small as a bug," muttered Pandora, conducting an imaginary conversation with her absent brother. "And squash you so *flat* that your insides would come out with a splat. . . ."

One and three-quarter Disposawands later, Pandora was getting the hang of magic. At first light, she'd crept out of bed, re-read the relevant instructions in the papers from the ring binder, and selected her first victim. Dangling from its hanger, adorned with layers of frills, lace, and petticoats, was her most hated dress. Cause of many wardrobe wars, the dress had perversely survived each and every one of Pandora's attempts to destroy it. "But *this* time . . . ," she gloated, circling it with one of her purloined wands, *"this* time . . ."

The lace on the collar lifted and stirred in the breeze caused by Pandora's passes with the wand. With a tiny metal clatter, it fell, complete with tiny metal hanger, onto the floor at her feet. Diminishing afterimages faded in its wake—identical dresses for eight-, seven-, six-, five-, four-, three-, two-, Damp-year-olds, babies, and newborns, each one smaller than the next, each one fading slowly away until, with a gasp, Pandora picked up the smallest version from the floor. "When I find Multitudina's babies, this will be just *perfect* for one of them," she said, holding the tiny thing in the palm of her hand.

Several hours later, Pandora's room had undergone a radical transformation. From the curtain poles hung two pocket-handkerchief-sized curtains. A miniature library of books the size of postage stamps huddled forlornly at the end of a large bookcase, lost in the vast space that now surrounded them. Pandora's wardrobe had become her new jewelry box and the bedroom floor was dotted with thumbnail-sized teddies and dolls. There had been a few casualties along the way—where she was going to sleep might present a problem since her bed was now the size of a matchbox, and CDs the size of pinheads were frankly useless, but Pandora was feeling triumphant.

"Easy peasy, lemon squeezy," she said. "*Now* for something trickier." She flung herself onto her bed, forgetting that it had been an early casualty of the learning process. There was a tiny crunch from beneath her leg. "First thing I'll try is matchsticks into mattresses," she muttered, picking out the splinters.

A Little Family History

Luciano Strega-Borgia breakfasted alone. He sat flanked by coffeepots, little dishes of apricot jam, platters of prosciutto, and enough croissants to feed a small army. However, the fact remained that his left ankle was chained to the table, and next to his plate was a document requiring his signature. Gazing out at the cypresses mirrored in the lake, he wondered if he'd ever see his wife and family again. His appetite deserted him as he remembered the morning he'd stormed out of StregaSchloss, all those weeks ago. . . .

It had started with bickering at breakfast.

He'd come downstairs to the kitchen where his family was eating breakfast. The table was already awash with milk. Damp was grizzling and Titus and Pandora were looking particularly glum. At the head of the table, his wife of many years, the beautiful Signora Strega-Borgia, sat with her head buried in the local paper. At the range, wearing a particularly black scowl, Marie Bain stood murdering a panful of scrambled eggs.

On seeing her father, Damp threw her hands in the air, sending her cereal bowl skidding off the table and across the floor. She bounced up and down in her clip-on baby seat, causing everything on the table to bounce up and down in tandem. Coffee and orange juice slopped out of cups and glasses. Cereal boxes toppled over and spilled their contents.

Serenely unaware of the squalor surrounding her, Signora Strega-Borgia stirred her coffee with the end of a pencil, licked it dry, and circled something in the paper.

Signor Strega-Borgia sat down at the breakfast table. Damp hurled her cup at him by way of welcome. Marie Bain placed a plate of blackened eggs in front of him.

"Dad, I've got a bit of a problem," said Titus.

"That's a major understatement," said Pandora, scattering sugar over her cereal, the surrounding tablecloth and, ultimately, the floor.

"Dad," said Titus, ignoring his sister, "you know you let me load Death & Destruction II onto your computer?"

"Titus, you are terminally boring, d'you know that?" interrupted Pandora. "All you ever do is talk about computers from the moment you open your eyes in the morning until—"

"Shut up, Pan," said Titus. "It's rude to interrupt."

"It's even ruder to bore the pants off everyone," mumbled Pandora, through a mouthful of Ricey Krispettes. Several Ricey Krispettes were launched floorward with each word.

Damp, her baby barometer sensing an impending storm, began to wail.

"Well, the problem is . . . Dad? Dad? Are you listening?"

"AAAARGH!" yelled Signor Strega-Borgia.

"Something wrong, darling?" said Signora Strega-Borgia, dropping her paper in the communal milk pool.

69

"TOO RIGHT, SOMETHING'S WRONG!" yelled Signor Strega-Borgia illogically.

Damp began to cry in earnest.

"Dad, look, I'm really sorry I crashed your computer, but it wasn't my fault," blurted Titus.

Signor Strega-Borgia leapt to his feet, causing his chair to crash backward onto the floor. "I've had it!" he shouted at his family. "I'm sick of living in a pigsty!" He waved at the table. "I'm sick of eating pig swill!" He hurled his plate at the wall. "And above all, I'm fed up to the back teeth with the lot of you!"

His family looked at him in dismay. In the background, Marie Bain curled up on the floor with the broken crockery and tried to make herself invisible. Above her head, scrambled eggs tracked slowly down the wall.

"Well . . . ," said Signora Strega-Borgia icily, "you know what you can do about that, don't you?"

"Mum . . . ," warned Pandora.

"Dad?" pleaded Titus. "Dad . . ."

"Mummy and Daddy need to have a little talk, darlings," said Signora Strega-Borgia, in an icy voice. "Why don't you all go upstairs while we sort ourselves out?" She fixed her children with a wide smile. Unfortunately, noted Titus, it wasn't the kind of smile that reached her eyes.

"Please don't argue?" he begged.

"Please go upstairs. Now. And take the baby," said Signora Strega-Borgia, standing up and opening the kitchen door.

In a hush full of unanswered questions, the children trooped out of the kitchen, followed by Marie Bain, who dabbed at her eyes with her apron and sniffed disapprovingly. The sound of their footsteps died away, leaving Signor Strega-Borgia and his wife in silence.

A faraway clock chimed the hour.

"Well . . . ," said Signora Strega-Borgia, sitting down and examining her fingernails.

"I'd best be off, then," said her husband, hoping that he didn't have to go.

"As you wish," said Signora Strega-Borgia, retrieving her newspaper from the milk pool. Her hands trembled and her eyes filled with tears, but she hid herself behind the soggy newsprint. It was this apparent lack of concern and frosty dismissal that made Signor Strega-Borgia's mind up.

"Don't expect me back for supper," he said, glaring at her bent head. His words failed to penetrate her chilly armor. "Or tomorrow," he added, from the door.

"Bye," said his wife, from behind the paper where her face was wet with tears. "Lock the gate after you. . . ."

With a massive attempt at injured dignity, Signor Strega-Borgia walked out on his life, his wife, and his family. And from there on, it had all been downhill.

Somewhere along the road, he'd taken a wrong turn and he hardly recognized his surroundings. Moreover, by then it was way past lunchtime and he was starving. The shoulders of his jacket were soaked, his trousers were splattered with mud, and his stomach growled incessantly.

When the sleek black Mercedes pulled up beside him, his hair was plastered to his skull and he felt he'd sunk as low as it was possible to go. As the passenger door opened, he'd had no idea just how much farther he still had to fall. . . .

The sound of voices from outside the window dragged him back to the present. In the early morning Italian sunlight, Signor

Strega-Borgia saw Pronto loading a violin case into the trunk of a large black car.

"Don't worry, Maestro," Pronto called to someone out of the field of Signor Strega-Borgia's vision. "It's time for them to face the music. When I finish, there won't be a single one left standing."

Signor Strega-Borgia puzzled over this statement as he helped himself to another cup of coffee. Was Pronto such a talented musician that his performances literally brought the house down? Or was it that his skill with a violin was such that his concert audiences knelt before him in adoration?

Drawing a finger slowly across his throat, Pronto climbed into the rear seat, and the car drew away, its tires crunching gravel and its black windows throwing back a reflection of the blank face of the palazzo. In one of those moments where something clicks and realization dawns, Signor Strega-Borgia suddenly understood. Maybe it had nothing to do with music, he thought as his legs turned to water and his heart leapt free of its moorings and flew into his mouth. Maybe Pronto was on a deadly mission? To StregaSchloss!

Hearing the front door slam and the heavy tread of approaching footsteps, Signor Strega-Borgia drained his coffee cup and picked up the document that lay beside his untouched breakfast. It appeared to be a will. In fact, it appeared to be *his* will. Hardly believing the evidence before his eyes, Signor Strega-Borgia read that as the trustee for his son, Titus, he had decided to make a few changes. . . . Clutching his throat, Signor Strega-Borgia scanned the document:

After much thought . . . due to the corrupting influence

> of vast sums of money . . . Titus too young to inherit
> . . . I, Luciano Strega–Borgia, being of sound mind . . .
> hereby decree . . . in the event of my death . . . going
> to leave everything I possess to . . .

"NEVER!" he shouted, just as Don Lucifer's hairy nostrils appeared, as was their habit, three seconds before the rest of his half brother.

"Never?" queried Don Lucifer, idly tapping the business end of a rather wicked-looking handgun.

"Um, yes, um, I was just saying I've never drunk a finer cup of . . . um, ah . . ." Luciano's words trailed off into silence.

The brothers' eyes met over the handgun. "When you've signed that thing," Don Lucifer remarked in a very matter-of-fact way, "I need you to have a look at my computer. It's got some kind of virus playing havoc with the mainframe."

"Lucifer, d'you think I'm a complete pushover? A total jelly that you can just shove around?"

Don Lucifer gazed impassively at his sibling. "Yup," he said, clicking the gun's safety catch to the off position, struck by the happy thought that the inhabitants of StregaSchloss would soon be dead, no matter what his jelly of a half brother did. "Don't be a fool, Luciano. Sign on the dotted line and then get downstairs and sort out my computer problem or, later on today, your precious son will have an unfortunate accident, resulting in his untimely demise. Guaranteed. So do as you're told, and don't waste any more of my time."

It's only money, Signor Strega-Borgia told himself as he signed away his stamp collection, his bank balance, Titus's inheritance, and most importantly, StregaSchloss, his home.

The thought of its acute vulnerability to invasion by Mafia thugs caused him to wish he'd installed a slightly more high-tech security system than a dungeonful of mythical beasts.

A vision of his beloved family under threat from a violin-bearing menace caused him to burst into tears. "Don't hurt them, Lucifer . . . PLEASE? I'll do anything, but just leave my family out of this, I beg you, pleeeeease. . . ." He fell sobbing to the carpet, in the knowledge that he was, indeed, a jelly.

E-rats Redux

Luciano Strega-Borgia hobbled along the deserted corridors of the palazzo, held at gunpoint by his brother, dimly aware that the floor had been newly polished with something that smelled vaguely of gasoline. Indeed the marble floors shone so much that they were slightly slippery underfoot. Don Lucifer stopped at a little door marked TUG and pushed. Not surprisingly, nothing happened. Don Lucifer clapped himself on the forehead, tugged, and entered.

Despite a total lack of human presence, the room seemed alive. Screens flickered, modems hummed and shrieked their strange peacock call, and the noise of spinning disks and coolant fans merged with excited squeakings and scrapings coming from one corner of the room.

"It's all yours." The Don indicated the room at large, and then grabbed Signor Strega-Borgia by the lapels. "And don't be so stupid as to try and get help. You e-mail the Carabinieri, the

FBI, the CIA, the Gendarmes, any form of police you like, and all the computers will crash instantly. It's been programmed to alert me if anyone so much as keys in 999. So don't even *think* about it. No calling for help, or you're fish food." He released his quaking half brother and smiled encouragingly. "The virus. The rats. That's what you're here for. Get it sorted, Luciano, there's a good boy." With this, Don Lucifer turned on his heels and walked out of the room, pushing the door shut behind him.

In a dazed state of obedience, Signor Strega-Borgia sought the source of the squeaking. Pulling up a chair, he sat in front of one screen that appeared to be running a most unusual screen saver. He looked more closely. That wasn't a screen saver. That was an infestation. Thirteen rat babies looked back at him through the glass. Beside them, a modem lit up and quietly exploded. The screen turned black and smoke began to leak apologetically from its rear.

"We have a problem," muttered Signor Strega-Borgia, turning to a fresh screen and keying in a set of commands.

>YOU'RE ABSOLUTELY RIGHT, LAMEBRAIN< agreed the computer.

/QUERY SOURCE/ typed Signor Strega-Borgia, ignoring the insult.

>THAT'S FOR ME TO KNOW, AND YOU TO FIND OUT< said the computer, aggravating things further by adding ten rows of asterisks, this being a computer's equivalent of sticking its tongue out and yelling Nya Nya, nah NYA NYA.

"So you don't wish to reveal your source, do you?" muttered Signor Strega-Borgia, and pressed five keys simultaneously. ￢

Immediately the screen went black, and almost immediately

lit back up again. >NO NEED TO BE QUITE SO BRUTAL< complained the computer, >VIOLENCE NEVER SOLVED ANYTHING<

"No," agreed Signor Strega-Borgia, "but a quick crash and reboot might bring you to your senses."

He typed /QUERY SOURCE/ again.

The computer replied with the equivalent of "Wild Horses Wouldn't Drag That Information from Me": >MMMMMMMMMMM< it said.

Signor Strega-Borgia typed /REBOOT? QUERY?/

>MMMMNYA POO< replied the computer, adding, >I'LL NEVER REVEAL MY SOURCES, NO MATTER WHAT. MMMMMMM<

Signor Strega-Borgia resorted to desperate measures. Opening a bottle of brown fizzy liquid abandoned by a previous operator, he held it over the air vents on the computer.

/RIGHT/ he typed. /COKE IN THE VENTS OR—SOURCE. QUERY?/

>YOU NASTY BIG LAMEBRAIN BRUTE< complained the computer. >MAY YOUR HARD DISK CEASE TO SPIN, AND ALL YOUR FILES RASP. MAY ALL YOUR CRASHES BE FATAL AND YOUR REBOOTS BE DOC MARTENS . . .<

/SOURCE. QUERY? OR ELSE/ typed Signor Strega-Borgia.

>OH VERY WELL, BRAWN OVER BRAIN. STREGA-SCHLOSS.CO.UK. HAPPY NOW?<

"WHAT?" screamed Signor Strega-Borgia.

The computer, not possessing a pair of ears, didn't respond.

/QUERY. ERROR, SURELY?/ typed Signor Strega-Borgia, his hands suddenly clammy on the keyboard.

>NOPE NEGATIVE NIX NOT! STREGASCHLOSS.CO.UK IT IS. MMMMMMMM< replied the computer, adding two rows of ampersands by way of salt in the wound.

"Titus," groaned Signor Strega-Borgia, slumping onto the keyboard. "What have you *done?*"

How had his only son sent an infestation of rats across the Internet and straight into his half brother's unbelievably complex computer system? And never mind how or even why, judging by Don Lucifer's threats, Titus could be in extreme danger. Feverishly, his fingers flying over the keys, Signor Strega-Borgia typed out a message.

titus@stregaschloss.co.uk

Titus
Something very wicked is about to arrive on your doorstep. Don't ask. just do what i say. Try and get your mum and your sisters down into the dungeon with the beasts, and stay there until . . .

What? Until what? Until he got home? That was becoming more unlikely by the minute. Signor Strega-Borgia wasn't coming home, not if his evil half brother had anything to do with it. He began again.

titus@stregaschloss.co.uk

Titus
i've been kidnapped by a psychopathic relative. don't worry.

On reflection, he removed the last bit.

Titus
I've been kidnapped and can't get home. i think you're all in grave danger as well. The best thing to do is panic.

This wasn't going at all well. He considered getting Titus to phone the police, but he knew that a twelve-year-old trying to tell the local Highland constabulary that he'd just had an e-mail from his estranged father saying that there was an unspecified threat on its way from somewhere unknown was *not* going to bring several officers in blue to the door of StregaSchloss. Plus, as his half brother had been at such pains to point out, if he so much as typed 999, or "police," the computer would alert Lucifer before it crashed. . . . Think, man, he beseeched himself. Ah, there it was, the kind of message that would convey the gravity of the situation in a fashion that his son might understand.

Titus
Aliens abducted me on my way to auchen-lochtermuchty and are about to launch an attack on stregaschloss. i would have come home sooner, but you know how uncool these beings with green antennae coming out of their foreheads can be.
Take the beasts and your sisters and your mum and get as far away from stregaschloss as possible. please. please? and be warned. the aliens will probably be armed and are definitely dangerous. be careful.
i love you,
dad
p.s. did you send thirteen rats down the modem?

Signor Strega-Borgia keyed in a row of X's and sat back, trembling. Onscreen a dialogue box appeared: SEND?
Signor Strega-Borgia hit the ENTER key with such force that

the plastic cracked and it divided in two, becoming the ENT and ER keys. Onscreen the dialogue box read: MESSAGE SENT >BUT YOU DIDN'T HAVE TO BE QUITE SO NEANDERTHAL<

Signor Strega-Borgia ignored this and began to chew his fingernails. On a nearby screen, twenty-six rat eyes glared pinkly out at him. They were assessing his food value (minimal), his general value to ratkind (zilch), and his intelligence (nonexistent since he hadn't brought any bacon rinds). Bored, the rats turned away and began to gnaw pixels by the dozen.

Damp on the Web

Mrs. McLachlan's raspberry muffins were good, thought Titus, rather too good, in fact. After eating more than his fair share (eight out of twelve), he headed upstairs to his computer. When the screen flickered into life, a dialogue box appeared with YOU HAVE MAIL on it.

"Spam," muttered Titus, under his breath, ignoring the announcement and loading *Death & Destruction II* into the CD-ROM.

The dialogue box politely made itself scarce, waiting until Titus had assembled his armies onscreen, equipped them with a bristling array of weaponry, and was just about to begin the assault on the peaceful kingdom of computer-generated Nettlefold. Titus paused, fingers hovering above the keyboard. There was that annoying dialogue box getting in the way again. All unknowing, the innocent citizens of the kingdom of Nettlefold slept on into oblivion. They remained unaware that the agent of their destruction was a large box hanging in the sky that bore the legend:

YOU STILL HAVE MAIL. THE KIND OF MAIL THAT DOESN'T LIE MEEKLY ON THE MAT WAITING TO BE OPENED. THIS IS MAIL WITH MENACES. IT DEMANDS TO BE READ, OR ELSE. . . .

Titus groaned. Not again. *Death & Destruction II* was always pulling this kind of stunt. The trouble was that it was such an aggressive game. Every time he loaded it, it tried to pick a fight with everything in its way—first the CD-ROM, then the RAM, then the processor. Maybe he'd try it again, later. In the meantime, out with *Death & Destruction II* and check the mailbox.

Titus sat back and waited. The dialogue box disappeared again, muttering darkly to itself. After a lot of whirring fans and little clicky noises from deep within the computer, a message appeared onscreen.

UNLESS YOU OPEN YOUR MAIL NOW, THIS COMPUTER WILL TURN INTO A LARGE WHITE BOX THAT HAS NO MEMORY OF BEING ANYTHING OTHER THAN A LARGE WHITE BOX.

"OK, OK. Chill out, would you?" groaned Titus, pressing ENTER. His eyes grew wide. "WHAT?" he yelled. "Dad? What is this rubbish?"

His fingers a blur on the keyboard, Titus replied:

dad@mafia.org.ital

For signor strega-borgia, missing father of Titus, abandoner of family, etc.
Dear Sir,
the rats belong to your daughter. perhaps

82

you'd like to ask HER how they got there?
anyway, aliens don't have antennae coming
out of their heads. That's SAD, dad. Think of
a better excuse. And none of this is my
fault.
  hope you're well,
  Your Son,
  Titus

He pressed ENTER, wiped a tear off the keyboard, and
reloaded *Death & Destruction II*. Nettlefold didn't stand a
chance.

Signor Strega-Borgia burst into dramatic tears when Titus's
message arrived onscreen. Immediately he responded:

  titus@stregaschloss.co.uk

  For Titus Strega-Borgia's eyes only. Master
of the mouse, genius of the joystick, beloved
only son of Luciano the low, dad the sad.
  My dear Titus,
  PEACE?
  Please forgive me—the alien idea was
pretty sad, I admit. However, it's not an
excuse. I was kidnapped, but by some rather
scary gangsters, not aliens, and I'm stuck in
a dungeon somewhere in the Italian countryside. Titus, I can't get home just yet. I'm not
sure, but i think one of the gangsters may
be on his way to StregaSchloss. Just in case,
could you lock all the doors and somehow

keep your mother and sisters (and yourself,
of course!) in the same room as Ffup, Knot,
and Sab. and Tock, too, if you can manage.

and stay away from the windows.

call me a paranoid old dad, but until I'm
back home to look after you all myself, do
me a favor and humor your ancient father,
huh? I miss you every day, and love you
lots.

hugs and more hugs,
Dad
P.S. Have you worked out how to trash
nettlefold yet?

There ... done. He'd struck the right balance between
giving a clear warning and not throwing Titus into a terror-
stricken panic. And he hadn't once mentioned police, so his
message wouldn't alert Lucifer's alarm system. Feeling faintly
smug, Signor Strega-Borgia carefully pressed ENT and ER
simultaneously, and sent his message winging out across the
Web. He sat back in his chair, wiping his streaming face with
his sleeve. For some reason, the air conditioning in the computer room appeared to be malfunctioning, but thankfully, the
pervasive smell of gasoline-based floor polish had gone.

Above the smoking remains of Nettlefold, a giant box hung in
the sky.

Titus sniffed as he typed in a message:

dad@mafia.org.ital

Dear Dad
Yeah, right, dad. So it's gangsters now, not

aliens with antennae? have the gangsters got
machine guns in violin cases as well? ha-ha.
get a life, dad. i'm 12 not 2. and if you
think i'm letting Sab, Tock, Ffup, and Knot
into my bedroom, you can think again.
they're not toilet-trained yet. Hurry up and
come home. We all miss you.
  Lots of love,
  Titus
  p.s. nettlefold is toast.

It was at this tender moment that Pandora threw open the
door to her brother's bedroom and announced that Titus, too,
was going the same way as the computer-generated kingdom
of Nettlefold.

"Titus, you're toast. You're history. You're about to be an
ex-Titus . . . ," she gloated, waving a disposable wand for
emphasis.

"Go *away*, Pandora," muttered Titus, his eyes not leaving the
screen. "I know where your rats went, and believe me, they're
not coming back."

Wearing a brand-new diaper, and modeling a dazzlingly
pink pair of overalls, Damp crawled into Titus's bedroom to check
if the face was still hungry. Titus and Pandora were too
engrossed in mutual slander to notice her crawling purposefully
toward the computer. Damp gazed upward at the CD-ROM
drawer in adoration. With an inaudible shriek from the hard
disk, *Death & Destruction II* crashed again, causing the CD
drawer to spring open and eject the quarrelsome disk. Damp
crawled closer for a good look. At this point, time appeared to
speed up and everything began to happen rather quickly.

on hearing the CD-ROM drawer open, and curious as to
her the bacon rinds were still inside, Multitudina made a
run for the computer. Behind Titus's back, Pandora began to
draw circles with her wand. Faster and faster until, just before
the final thrust, she stepped forward, tripped over the running
Multitudina, and aimed her final blast not at Titus but at
Damp.

Titus, fingers poised over the keyboard, about to send his letter to dad@mafia.org.ital, gave an enormous sneeze that
launched his miniaturized baby sister into orbit. Currently
about the size of a small thumbnail, Damp was blown into the
open CD drawer and spun upward into the modem.

As the sneeze left Titus's nose, his fingers reflexively pressed
ENTER. Onscreen a dialogue box informed him: MESSAGES SENT.
It was Pandora's terrible scream that told him what he had
really sent.

Pronto Gets Help

Flying from Italian sunshine into Scottish drizzle had done nothing to improve Pronto's mood. Dressed for a kinder climate, he was soaked to the skin by the time he arrived at the dingy dockside offices of the Edinburgh branch of Rent-a-Thug. His shoes squelched, his suit dripped black dye, and his cell phone was suspiciously soggy. Across the desk from him, a fat man in a pinstripe suit rolled his eyes heavenward, and wheezed into a telephone receiver buried under his many chins. "Danny the Fox is doing a six-to-ten stretch, huh? What about Sid the Slash?"

A polite knock at the door, and the fat man's secretary poked her head round. "There's a Mr. Machiavelli from Garrotes R Us in reception for you, boss," she trilled.

The fat man gave her the thumbs-up sign.

"And that consignment of Uzi nine millimeters has just arrived—shall I unpack them now?"

The fat man nodded and waved her away with an impatient hand. "Too bad," he murmured down the telephone. "He should have stuck to his knives, our Sid. Plastic explosives are such unforgiving stuff. . . ." He paused and scratched his armpit in a thoughtful kind of way. "So what can you do for me? What've you got left? Yeah, I need one more for this very special client." He grinned an unpleasant gold-capped grin across the desk at Pronto. "Yeah, the usual arrangement, yeah, that's right. Half up front, the remainder when the job's done. So . . . who have you come up with? Attila? Attila what? What sort of a name is that? Hang on, I'll ask my client."

The fat man gagged the telephone with one vast paw and leaned across the desk to Pronto. "My friend says he's got a real nutter for you. Guy by the name of Attila the Bun."

Pronto raised one eyebrow.

"Yeah, I know, but it gets better. Apparently, he wears a full rabbit suit all the time—hence the nickname, but my friend says he's one of the best in the business."

Pronto raked the fat man with a disbelieving stare.

The fat man oozed back across the desk and slumped in his chair. "Look, pal, you can take it or leave it. S'up to you. All I know is you want four professional personnel-terminators for a job up in the Highlands, no questions asked, *and* you want them *now*, ASAP, pronto, toot sweet. . . ."

"How did you get my name?" interrupted Pronto.

"Look, Toots, or whatever you call yourself, get this—I can't find you four expert terminators at such short notice. Three I can do, four, no can do. Either you take this Tillybun bloke and we've got a deal, or you're stuck with the three we got."

Pronto decided.

"Right, squire, we've got a deal," said the fat man, retrieving the receiver from his clammy fist and replacing it under his chins. "OK, we cut the rabbit in. Usual place, give my client an hour to find himself a motor. Yeah, yeah, he knows the form. Unmarked bills, in the left luggage at the station. Yeah. You too. Bye." Sweating copiously, the fat man replaced the receiver and collapsed in his chair. Mopping his face with a lace-trimmed handkerchief, he began to draw a map for Pronto.

Exactly one hour later, Pronto arrived in a rented van at the agreed rendezvous. Edinburgh was in the grip of festival fever, and the chosen location was thronged with tourists, street performers, jugglers, acrobats, and, regrettably, more than one fully dressed rabbit.

Pronto had no trouble spotting his three experts. They stood in a group, wearing sunglasses, black suits, and deep scowls. They were far more conspicuous in the crowd of brightly dressed, happy festival-goers than their companion in his rabbit costume. As instructed by the fat man, Pronto stuck his head out of the van window, pretending to ask directions from passersby. "Anyone know where I can find a theater group called Terminator Four?" he yelled.

Three large guys began to move in his direction. Nearby, a well-dressed rabbit detached himself from an audience of small children and began to hop toward the van. One small boy appeared to be reluctant to say goodbye. He clung determinedly to the rabbit's leg, his face crumpling with the effort.

The three large men climbed into the rear of the van, holding the door open for their lopsidedly hopping companion.

"Get OFF," the rabbit growled at the leechlike child. "Leggo, or I'll . . ."

Abruptly the child let go before he could complete his threat. The rabbit bounded into the back of the van, slamming the door behind him.

Across the street, an apprentice piper, in full Highland dress, began to coax the opening bars of "Auld Lang Syne" from his bagpipes. It sounded awful, but it masked the squeal of brakes and the child's earsplitting wail, "That bunny's got a GUN!"

Swerving to overtake a trailer, Pronto shuddered at the memory. In the passenger seat beside him now, the rabbit twiddled dials on the radio, played with the heater controls, and wound the window up and down, all the while keeping up an endless flow of chatter.

"Know what this motor needs, eh?" he asked of the company in general. "Needs some of them furry dice, dunnit?" he said to no one in particular. "My mate's motor, now there's a really cool set of wheels—he's got the dice, tinted windows, alloy wheels, sound system big enough ter blow the windows out. . . ."

"How useful," muttered Pronto. "No vehicle should be without one."

"That's what I mean," continued the rabbit. "And he's got satellite navigation, turbocharged twin-cam fuel-injected whatchamacallits . . ."

"*Really?*" said Pronto, investing that one word with every ounce of sarcasm at his disposal. "And your 'friend,' what does he do?"

"Eh? What d'you mean, 'what does he do'?"

"I mean," said Pronto, speaking very slowly and carefully. "What. Does. He. Do. For. A. Living. Your. Friend?"

"Uhh. I get your meaning. He doesn't do nothing for a living. He's dead."

"Oh dear, how sad," said Pronto insincerely.

The van began to slow down as they approached a vast rusting bridge. Pronto riffled through his pockets and turned round in his seat. "Look, we have to pay to cross this toll bridge. Has anyone got any change? I only have big notes."

"I haven't any pockets, pal," said the rabbit, stating the obvious.

Mutters from the rear of the van told Pronto that, like him, everyone was carrying either credit cards or rolls of big notes.

"Couldn't we just drive straight through the barrier?" said the rabbit hopefully.

"No, we could *not*," growled Pronto. "We are trying not to draw any attention to ourselves. Here we are on a clandestine mission to some Highland fortress, intent on rubbing out a boy and anyone else that sees us do it. If we crash through the barrier, chances are we'll arrive at our destination with a police escort."

The van rolled to a halt in front of the toll barrier. Pronto wound down his window and extended his arm with a £100 note at the end of it.

"Haven't you got anything smaller?" the toll collector asked in disgust, "I haven't got change for *that*."

"Tell him to keep the change," said the rabbit. "And hurry it up, will ya? I need the bog."

"Will you shut *up* and let me deal with this," hissed Pronto. "He's hardly likely to forget several men and a rabbit who told him to keep £99.20 change, is he?"

"I can't wait much longer," moaned the rabbit to himself.

"You've no idea how long it takes to get this rabbit costume undone. . . . I'm gonna burst."

A line of bridge traffic began to form behind the van. The toll collector stuck his head round the door of his booth, the better to address them. "You'll just have to wait," he yelled. "Daddy Warbucks here hasn't anything smaller than a hundred-pound note, and I'll have to get some more change." Grumbling to himself, he strolled slowly off in the direction of the other tollbooths, holding the banknote out in front of him as if it was covered in plague bacteria.

Minutes dragged past. By now, the rabbit was jiggling frantically on his seat, causing the entire van to bounce up and down. "Oh, oh, oh. My bladder can't cope. I need a pee NOW—ow, ow, ow, it's like trying to stop Niagara Falls . . . urrrgh . . . hurry up, hurry up, hurry up."

The toll collector was deep in conversation at a faraway booth where his ancient colleague was slowly counting out £99.20 in pennies. From time to time, they glanced leisurely over to where the van was rocking back and forth, muffled screams coming from its interior.

To the amusement of the occupants in the long line of waiting cars, the van at the head of the line suddenly stopped bouncing and ejected one of its passengers. What was going on? The ejectee appeared to be attempting to divest himself of a large rabbit suit. He appeared to be in something of a tearing hurry. No? No. The rabbit had changed his mind.

The rabbit was now waddling back to the van, his furry legs held apart, leaving a trail of wet rabbit footprints on the tarmac behind him.

The toll collector shuffled back to his booth, effortfully

dragging a large canvas bag in which clinked £99.20 in coins. He stuck his head into the van, recoiled abruptly, and said, "Phhwoah. What's that *smell*? Did someone die in there while I was off getting your money?" He roared with laughter at his own wit and began to count out Pronto's change.

Several miles up the road, they stopped at a service station and bought four cans of air freshener. Several miles after that, they stopped at a pull-off and sprayed the rabbit. Shortly thereafter, the roads narrowed considerably. A series of s-curves and steep dips conspired to make everyone feel very queasy indeed. Everyone, that is, except the rabbit. He was quite happy; his costume had dried off nicely, he'd found an excellent heavy-metal station on the radio, and was rolling the window up and down in time to the beat.

"OPEN THE WINDOW!" yelled the three men in the back as the van lurched and rolled around another corner.

Several miles later, they stopped in the middle of nowhere and tied the rabbit to the roof rack.

A Wee Hot Toddy

ith the feeling that she might have lost several brownie points by tripping up her owner, Multitudina sneaked downstairs, back to the cellar. The smell of defrosted and rotting food had grown stronger since her last visit. A reeking lagoon surrounded the once-glacial freezer. I'm not tempted, Multitudina told herself firmly. Last time I sipped at *that* particular watering hole, my nose got fried. She gave the lake a wide berth and continued on her travels. Somewhere in this huge house, she thought, her stomach growling, there must be something for a mother-to-be to eat.

The rain had finally stopped, and weak sunshine trickled in through the kitchen windows. Mrs. McLachlan glared at Sab, Ffup, and Knot, who huddled round the kitchen table.

"There were *four* left," she said, tapping the muffin tray for emphasis. "And now there are none."

The beasts sighed sympathetically.

"I turned my back on them for one minute," she continued, "one minute while I heated up a wee hot toddy for the Signora, and when I turned round . . ."

Sab licked his lips nervously. Ffup stifled a belch with one leathery wing. Mrs. McLachlan stared at them. Knot lolloped out of the kitchen, leaving a half-eaten bunny slipper on the chair behind him.

"Did he do it?" demanded Mrs. McLachlan. "All *four* raspberry muffins? What a *pig*. After that enormous dinner he ate last night."

"Blaark," said Sab, holding his feathery stomach.

"Don't feel well," groaned Ffup, clutching his scaly one.

Mrs. McLachlan opened the door to the kitchen garden. "Not on the *herbs*," she warned as Sab and Ffup bolted past her. "Oh well . . . never mind, they'll wash."

Five minutes later, they returned, both looking rather pale and ill. "Must have been the smocked hiccup," whispered Ffup, wincing at the memory.

"Now I know why they're called Brussels splats," added Sab darkly.

Signora Strega-Borgia huddled under her bedcovers, a trail of tissues leading from the bathroom to her pillow. A fit of sneezing had left her as limp as an overcooked haddock, her throat felt as if she'd eaten a bowl of razor blades, and her nose ran like an Olympic athlete.

There was a discreet tap at the bedroom door, and Mrs. McLachlan breezed in, bearing a little tray on which something steamed. "Good morning, dear," she said, setting the tray down on a squelching pile of used tissues. "I've brought you a Morangie-Fiddach special. Three spoonfuls of heather honey, the juice of a lemon, both warmed together with three cloves, a cinnamon stick, and a blade of mace . . . oh, and did I mention? Three glasses of the finest whisky."

She watched in approval as Signora Strega-Borgia drained the mug in several swallows. "Nnngg," said Signora Strega-Borgia, as her eyes crossed and perspiration broke out on her forehead.

Mrs. McLachlan plumped pillows, smoothed the quilt, and tucked her employer in. "S'got," slurred Signora Strega-Borgia, flapping a hand at the empty mug, "s'got a kick like a mule . . . jusht closhe m'eyes forra bit. . . ." She slumped deeper into the pillows and began to snore.

Mrs. McLachlan drew the curtains shut, piled the tray with soggy tissues, and tiptoed out of the room. "Is the wee one with you, Titus?" she called, heading downstairs.

Titus opened his bedroom door just enough to poke his head round. "She's playing in the computer," he said truthfully.

Satisfied, Mrs. McLachlan descended to the kitchen.

Arachnids with Attitude

Titus closed his bedroom door and turned the key in the lock. Across the room, Pandora chewed her fingernails and stifled a sob.

"What are we going to do, Titus? How do we get Damp back?"

"We can't," Titus said baldly.

"We *must* be able to," wailed Pandora.

"It's like posting a letter," explained Titus. "Once you've *sent* something, you can't stick your hand into a postbox and pull it back out. . . ."

"You can wait till the postman unlocks the postbox, and ask him to fish your letter out. . . ."

"It's not the same thing," said Titus, running his hands through his hair. "We have to find out where she's gone, what address she's gone to, and then ask them to send her back."

"We're talking about her as if she's a parcel," sobbed Pandora. "She's a *baby*."

"She's a *lost* baby," said Titus. "And we have to find her before someone else does."

"What d'you mean *we*?" said Pandora, in between mouthfuls of fingernails. "I don't know anything about computers or the Internet."

They gazed at the screen, each lost in their own thoughts. "Neither do I, really," admitted Titus. "The Internet's like a big web, Pandora. It's absolutely vast. Colossal. Humungous. And somewhere, out there, on one of the millions of strands, is our baby sister."

Pandora groaned and rolled back on Titus's bed. She stared at the ceiling, tears rolling down her face, aware of what little hope they had of retrieving Damp. "Poor baby," she wept. "Lost on the Web. Stuck, like a . . . a fly, waiting helplessly for . . ."

"You called?" said a voice. Spinning down from the ceiling came a vast hairy spider.

Titus leapt backward as Tarantella touched down on his monitor. She paused, flexing all eight of her furry legs, and smiling at him with her aggressively pink lips. "YEEEEUCHH," he said, flapping her away. "Is she *still* alive? I thought I'd killed her years ago."

Tarantella hip-hopped closer, stopping to cup her chin in one of her legs and gaze at this impudent human. "What's his problem?" she asked Pandora.

"He's got several," said Pandora. "But mainly, he's got a thing about spiders."

"AAARGH—a *talking* spider," squeaked Titus. "When did it

learn to speak? And wear *lipstick*? EURCHH. Gross. Kill it, Pandora." He climbed onto a chair and curled himself up into a spider-proof ball.

"Titus. Chill out. She's only a spider," sighed Pandora.

"AAARGH—a talking *child*," mocked Tarantella. "Yeurk. Urg. Disgusting. And it's a *male* one too. . . . Kill it, Pandora."

"Tarantella. Titus," said Pandora, introducing one to the other. "Do shut up, both of you. Listen, this is *really* important. We need you, Tarantella. Yes, *we*," she added, quelling Titus with a glare. "Tarantella knows about webs; you know about computers. Together you might be able to find Damp."

"Is Damp the small wet thing that wears a toilet round her middle?" asked Tarantella, scuttling up a chair leg to face Pandora.

"Yes. Our four-legged baby sister," said Pandora. "She's lost on the biggest web ever."

"How big?" said Tarantella, producing a tiny lipstick and applying it to her mouthparts.

"Urrgh. Aaak. Lipstick . . . ," gagged Titus.

"Shut *up*, Titus," said Pandora. "The biggest ever," she continued to the spider, "stretching all the way around the world, and back."

"Lots of flies," murmured Tarantella, licking her lips.

"More than you could eat in a lifetime," said Pandora, adding, "and . . . it's all Multitudina's fault."

"That verminous baggage," spat Tarantella. "High time she donated her miserable carcass to medical science."

"We're straying off the point, Pan," warned Titus. "Time's flying and here you are rubbishing rodents while Damp wanders the Web."

"You don't mind if I wrap her before I bring her back?" said Tarantella, sidling toward the modem.

"Just don't accidentally eat her on the way home," said Pandora, beginning to twirl her Disposawand.

Titus instantly turned pale.

"What a revolting idea." Tarantella rolled her eyes in disgust. "Have you any idea how putrid human beings taste?" Her voice diminished as her tennis ball body shrank to the size of a period. Spitting delicately on the keyboard, she sprang into the air and vanished into the open drawer of the CD-ROM. Her disembodied voice filtered out. "Terrible compared to a nice plump bluebottle . . . or a sun-dried daddy longlegs . . . mmm . . . deee-licious. So thoughtful of you to leave one in here for me. . . ." There was a tiny crunch as Tarantella bit into a mummified fly wing she'd discovered in a corner of the modem.

In a dreamy state of revolted fascination, Titus pressed ENTER.

A Warm Welcome

An ornately carved metal gate barred the road to StregaSchloss. It bore a sign that read:

WARNING
Trespassers will be
a. served for breakfast
b. turned into frogs
c. forced to eat Brussels sprouts

Scowling, Pronto braked hard, threw the van into reverse, and backed down the road till he came to a patch of level ground shaded by some dusty chestnut trees. "From now on, we go on foot," he said, climbing down from the driver's seat and slouching to the rear of the van to unlock the back doors.

The three men in black unfolded their stiff legs and climbed out. Pronto retrieved his violin case from a rack inside the van and undid its clasps. Inside, nestled cozily on golden plush, lay a small machine gun. Pronto removed this, ripping away the plush to reveal several magazines of bullets. Threading these into the rapid-load cartridge, he made several clicks and snaps of a sort commonly associated with Being Up to No Good.

From the roof of the van, a muffled moan reminded him of his forgotten colleague. "Release the rabbit, would you?" he muttered to one of the men in black.

The man obeyed promptly, cutting the rabbit free with a wicked-looking knife. The rabbit slid off the roof and began to complain.

"You could have killed me with that stunt, you know," he moaned. "What if I'd fallen off?"

"Listen, Bun," hissed the knife-wielder, "one more peep out of you and you'll find yourself in pieces, shrink-wrapped in little Styrofoam trays in the refrigerated section of your local supermarket. Do I make myself clear?" He thrust a well-used handgun into the rabbit's paws and turned on his heel. Trailing a peach-scented cloud, Pronto and the posse tiptoed up the drive to StregaSchloss.

In the late afternoon sun, a great stillness hung over the house, as if the stone itself was basking in the warmth. Innocent of the impending threat, StregaSchloss, with its total absence of alarms and high-tech security systems, represented a burglar's dream venue. Nobody appeared at windows or doors, no guard dogs lunged at the end of leashes, and the front door stood ajar. There was, however, a long streak of something green and gelatinous smeared across the low bridge over the moat.

The rabbit stroked the muzzle of his handgun and scowled into the sun.

"Not exactly security-conscious, are they?" whispered one of the men in black.

"Right," said Pronto to the knife-wielder. "You, by the front door as lookout; you, round the back; and you and the rabbit, in with me through the front door." Pronto's black-shod foot made contact with the green glop decorating the moat. Immediately the smell of peach air freshener was overcome by something infinitely more unpleasant. The man posted to the back of the house sat down hurriedly on the edge of the moat.

"I feel sick," he muttered. "What is that *smell*?"

"Oh here we go again," moaned the rabbit. "Wait for it. . . ."

"Is that youse?" hissed the knife-wielder, swiveling round from his station by the front door. "If you've done something in your breeches again, I'm going to install ventilation in yon bunny costume."

"Cool it," muttered Pronto, glaring at his besmirched shoe. "It's not the rabbit, it's this green stuff."

"I'd hate to meet whatever did that," said the man at the front door, picking his teeth with his knife blade.

Gazing nervously around themselves, Pronto and his posse neglected to look upward. On wobbly wings, Ffup was on the home flight. Whatever had been in last night's smocked hiccup was responsible for the worst case of dragon diarrhea he'd encountered in 600 years. Ffup was hoping to make it back to his dungeon without another recurrence, but as his wings bore him closer to home, he realized that this was not to be. . . .

"Bombs away!" he yelled, swooping low over StregaSchloss. He saw little figures on the ground fleeing from the large green projectile that was speeding their way.

"And a direct hit, if I'm not mistaken," he observed to himself.

With a tremendous slapping sound, Ffup's digestive over-load landed on a human target. There was a scream, a ghastly choking sound, and then silence.

Close to the epicenter, the man on the edge of the moat groaned deeply, sank his face into his hands, and began to rock backward and forward, clutching his machine gun and moaning as he did so. In the reeds at the far side of the moat, something stirred. Something that hadn't eaten a nanny for weeks, never mind a gangster. . . .

"Come on," commanded Pronto, breathing shallowly through his mouth. He stepped carefully round the vast green puddle at the front door. "We've got a job to do. No time for sentimentality. Hey. You," he pointed to the man by the moat. "Take over at the door."

"This wasn't in the contract," muttered the rabbit, his tongue suddenly freed by the demise of the knife-wielder. "No one warned *me* about low-flying dragon poo. No one, come to think of it, so much as mentioned dragons." Regarding the slimy body of his fallen colleague with horror, he followed Pronto into StregaSchloss. As the front door closed behind them, there came a loud splash as Tock discovered the gastronomic delights of raw gangster with a light garnish of machine gun.

The Hot Toddy Revisited

Low bars of afternoon sunshine slanted through the windows of StregaSchloss, doing little to dispel the atmosphere of gloom in Titus's bedroom. Unaware that their home was being invaded, Titus and Pandora sat in front of the computer screen. Titus felt awful. No matter which keys he pressed or files he opened, he couldn't find a way to locate Damp. Who am I trying to kid, he thought, sending a spider off down a modem into the mother of all webs? There's no *way* Tarantella'll find her. Face facts, pal, you're in trouble. You need bigger, more qualified help than a talking spider with a knowledge of terrestrial webs. . . .

Pandora gazed hopelessly into space. Her eyes focused on nothing as she chewed her last fingernail, trying not to start crying again. It's hopeless, she thought, we don't know what we're doing, Tarantella doesn't know where she's going, and Damp is probably lost forever. At this point, a vast wave of unhappiness swept over her, and she began to cry.

"Come *on*, Pandora," said Titus, wrapping an arm round his weeping sister. "We've got to face up to this. We need help."

Pandora's shoulders heaved.

"I'm going to tell Mum," Titus decided. "We can't handle this on our own."

Pandora's face appeared from behind her hands. Her eyes were pink, her nose ran, and her face was awash with tears. Titus doubted if it was humanly possible to look more miserable than his sister did at this moment. "Mum'll kill us," she whispered.

"Yup," agreed Titus, adding illogically, "but it'll be worth it to get Damp back."

"I'd do *anything* for that," sobbed Pandora.

"I *know*," said Titus, patting her back. "I'd do anything as well. She may be small and smelly, but she's *ours*, our baby sister."

"I miss her," howled Pandora, "even if she does take up all the bed."

"Me too," said Titus, his voice wobbling dangerously near to a sob. "Don't worry, Mum'll know what to do."

They stood outside Signora Strega-Borgia's bedroom, unsure of what to do next.

"You go first," said Titus. "You tell her."

"I'd rather you did," said Pandora.

"No, you tell her. You look *really* sad, she'll feel sorry for you," said Titus. "I look too normal, she'll think I don't care or something."

"MUM," sobbed Pandora, opening the door and starting to cry again. "Mum, something awful's happened. . . ."

Signora Strega-Borgia lay across her bed, a huge smile on

her face. She hiccuped, rolled onto her stomach, and fell onto the carpet, still smiling. "Oopsee," she said. "Shilly me. Shorry, darlingsh, Mummy's a bit shquiffy." For some reason, she appeared to find this enormously funny, and she rolled around on the carpet, roaring with laughter at her own wit.

Titus was horrified. "She's *drunk*," he hissed.

"Legleshh," agreed Signora Strega-Borgia, overhearing Titus's comment. "Drunk ash a shkunk. Wheeeee. Dear Mishish McLachlan and her hot toddy. Hot toddy. Soddy soddy, lots of toddy." She rolled to a halt at Pandora's feet and gazed upward at her daughter. "Wosha matter, darling?" she slurred. "You look a bit upshet. Bit shad? Down in the dumpsh?"

Pandora sank to her knees, still crying. "We've lost Damp," she began. "On the computer. I borrowed one of your spells, shrank Damp, and she ended up in the modem."

Titus looked at Pandora in admiration. She didn't mention my part in the disappearance of Damp, he thought. Mind you, he added, nor did she mention Multitudina's. . . .

"Modem, shmodem," said Signora Strega-Borgia unhelpfully. "That'sh your father'sh department. Me, I'm jusht a shimple witshhh, no interesht whatshoever in technoloshy."

"But Mum—we've lost *Damp*. She's vanished."

Pandora watched as her mother heaved herself across the carpet and hauled herself inelegantly back into bed. She picked up her pillow, gazed at it in apparent adoration, and kissed it tenderly before placing it on the bed beside her. With a little smile, she pulled the covers up to her chin. "Ashk your father," she said, closing her eyes. "He'sh good with computersh. And don't worry about Damp," she added, patting her pillow lovingly. "She'sh quite shafe here with Mummy, aren't you, pet?"

Titus and Pandora stood unbelievingly by their mother's bedside, watching until her heavy breathing turned into loud snores. In a state of shock, they tiptoed backward out of the bedroom. In floods of tears, Pandora fled to the bathroom.

"She was *drunk*," muttered Titus as he stormed upstairs. "I've *never*, ever seen her do that before. She was disgustingly, dreadfully, horribly, revoltingly DRUNK!" Titus burst into tears and sat down abruptly on the stairs. I can't handle this, he thought. First, Dad does a bunk, then Damp vanishes, and now . . . He gripped one of the balustrades as if he wished to throttle it. Fathers aren't supposed to leave their children, baby sisters aren't supposed to shrink and vanish into the ether, and mothers are definitely *not* supposed to get drunk. Holding the balustrade for support, Titus stood up. Wearily, as if he carried a huge weight on his shoulders, he wiped his eyes with his sleeve and headed for his bedroom. Closing the door firmly behind him, Titus looked around himself. His bedroom afforded little comfort. No solutions leapt out at him from the overcrowded bookcase. He didn't own any manuals on how to find missing babies. The afternoon sun shining in through the window failed to raise his spirits, and it only served as a reminder that Damp had been missing for several hours. His unmade bed seemed to be the sleeping place of some other, younger version of himself. The model airplanes dangling from the ceiling on dusty threads were made by some other, younger Titus. With the disappearance of his father and now Damp, Titus felt that his childhood was over. Something has to be done, he resolved. Help has to be found.

He sat down heavily in the chair in front of his computer and began to type a message to his father.

signor strega-borgia at dad@mafia.org.ital
Dad,
We're in trouble. Damp is lost, mum is drunk, and we need your help. Please can you come home immediately? And no more sad kidnap stuff. this is serious.
Love,
Titus

He pressed ENTER, but nothing happened. He pressed it again, but still nothing. No reassuring MESSAGE SENT box, just his own letter hanging there on the blue screen.

"Oh GREAT!" yelled Titus. "Just what I need. Come *on*. Do it for me. Just this once. *Please*."

Unknown to Titus, inside the modem a minute speck of fly wing dropped by the outgoing Tarantella lay across a vital part of the circuitry. This was causing Titus's message to pause in its journey, shriek to a halt, perform a speedy U-turn and head back to base with the happy news that the information super-highway was now blocked. Also unknown to Titus, this was one of those occasions when a swift thwack to the modem would have solved the problem. However, Titus had been brought up to seek logical solutions rather than those of brute force. In vain, he opened files, scrolled through Help directories, and trawled through computer manuals before laying his head on the keyboard and conceding defeat.

His sister was lost, his mother drunk, and his father unreachable. Concluding that there was nothing more that *he* could do, Titus loaded *Death & Destruction II* and began to plan his assault on Nettlefold.

Tarantella Does the Biz

Routed from **stregaschloss.co.uk** to **dad@mafia .org.ital**, Damp had one brief glimpse of her father's face before being whizzed off to the Web site for The Really Authentic Italian Food Company, known to its many clients worldwide as **spag.bol@mamma**.

Here was the place where you logged on to order pasta by the square mile. Here was where you could, should you wish, order up a pizza the size of the Coliseum.

Damp huddled in a corner of a monitor and looked out. Launched onto the Internet before lunchtime, she was now extremely hungry. The sight of so much food reminded her that she'd missed a meal. Wishing to share this discovery, she pressed her face up against the glass of the screen and began to grizzle. This failed to produce the desired result. No one scooped her up and bore her off to the kitchen, bib, and bowl. Damp turned up her volume a bit. Nobody noticed. Resorting to desperate measures, Damp flung herself around, thrashing her arms and legs, and uttered a brain-curdling shriek. Unfortunately, since she was the size of an atom, her best efforts were little louder than a whisper.

Her tiny body connected with an outgoing e-mail, and before she could blink, she found herself once more hurtling along the information superhighway like a human tumbleweed. Damp closed her eyes, opened her mouth, and howled. She whizzed along telephone wires, under the sea, along deep-sea communication cables, and occasionally was bounced up into outer space via satellites. Lights flashed past, electricity hummed, and computers shrieked like strangulated peacocks. Damp was thoroughly dizzy and deafened. Abruptly she came to a near standstill. She swung back and forth, at first in a wide arc, and then slower and slower in decreasing swings till finally she came to a complete halt.

A voice spoke. A friendly, furry, almost familiar voice. "Damplette!" it said. "Little Dampy-Pops! She of the diapered derriere. Oh, the *trouble* I've had trying to find you. I've been to banks in Bogotá, nuclear bunkers in Nevada, supermarkets in Surrey, and it was by sheer chance that I fancied some fettuccine with flies for lunch and found you here. . . . My mission, should I choose to accept it, is to return you to your siblings who, even as we dangle here on the World Wide Web, are sitting weeping, willing your safe return, wailing, and waiting to welcome you home."

Damp opened her eyes for a quick peek at the owner of the voice. Overhead, a gigantic spider smiled down at her. Damp instantly squeezed both eyes shut.

"Awww. C'mon, small," Tarantella coaxed. "I *know* I've got

eight legs and probably more hair than you've had in your life-time, but really, I'm on *your* side." She patted Damp's head reassuringly.

Damp flinched and squeezed her eyes even tighter shut.

"Oooh, baby," crooned Tarantella, "how about a lullaby?"

> *Poor little Damper,*
> *squashed in a Pamper,*
> *shrunk to the size of a bug.*
> *Along came a spider*
> *and dangled beside her*
> *and gave her a huge hairy hug.*

Damp burst into tears.

"Oh, I'm sorry. Sorrysorrysorry," cried Tarantella. "I didn't mean to frighten you. Don't cry, you'll short-circuit the Web. C'mon, pet, just think of me as a black woolly rug, and climb on board. . . ."

A little howl escaped Damp's lips.

"Oh dear. Desperate measures for desperate times," muttered Tarantella, beginning to spin.

Damp sat, eyes squinched shut, mouth compressed to a rose-bud pucker, trying to ignore the fact that she was being steadily wrapped in spider silk.

"The problem with the younger generation . . . ," panted Tarantella as she spun around the baby, ". . . is that you still buy into that Miss Muffet stuff. Haven't you heard of *Charlotte's Web,* or *James and the Giant Peach?*" She stood back to admire her handiwork. "Purrfect," she crooned, tucking the silk-swaddled baby under one leg. "And now . . ."

She stepped backward, onto the cyberspace equivalent of the

fast lane, and was immediately swallowed up in traffic. "WHEEEEEEEE!"

They crossed continents, traversed oceans, and navigated through outer space, and one hour later, at an indecent speed, were bounced into StregaSchloss. Crawling out of the modem and into the CD-ROM, Tarantella paused in the drawer and listened.

She could make out two voices. The one belonging to Titus sounded breathless and scared. The other, unknown, sounded aggressive and very close at hand. It said, *"Buon giorno,* Titus. Your uncle Lucifer sends you this greeting."* A loud bang and a scream convinced the spider that she should stay where she was. Chewing thoughtfully on the speck of fly wing that she had dropped on her outward journey, Tarantella looked down at her cocooned charge. Damp was oblivious to her surroundings and had fallen asleep during the journey home. The spider was no stranger to motherhood, even if the child appeared to be short of six legs. She patted Damp with a hairy leg, hugged her closer, and settled down to wait until it was safe to emerge. Beneath her, the circuitry in the computer sprang to life. Without a manual or even a Help directory, Tarantella had fixed Titus's computer problem. She'd simply eaten it.

A Gory Bit

No sounds penetrated the walls of the dungeon at
StregaSchloss. It was here, amid the restful drip of water
on stone, that Latch frequently took his afternoon nap.
Stretched out on a pile of straw, with the day's paper across his
face, he was blissfully unaware that StregaSchloss was under
siege.

Nearby, Sab was too involved with his own discomfort to
notice anything amiss. His stomach growled and rumbled, trying vainly to digest the previous night's smoked hiccup.

In a far corner, Ffup groaned in his sleep. The dragon had
staggered back to his bed in the dungeon, aware that he might
be in disgrace after his earlier bombing mission had buried a
visitor to StregaSchloss under a mound of green goo.

On Sab's return dungeonward, he'd found Tock on the
Schloss doorstep, polishing off the remains of Ffup's goo and
complaining about the lumpy bits. The crocodile smacked his

lips and paused to remove machine-gun fragments from between his teeth. The shredded remains of a black suit littering the moatside seemed to indicate that Tock had found a pudding to follow his main course.

"Great sauce, this," he had said, "but could we sieve out the metal bits next time?"

Just remembering this conversation was enough to make Sab's stomach churn. Rolling his eyes to the ceiling, the griffin turned himself back into stone. Instantly all activity in his stomach ceased. A slow smile spread across his granite muzzle. His thoughts turned to mountaintops, to pebbles and basalt. Latch's snores and the steady drip of water down the dungeon walls faded from the griffin's consciousness.

A shadow fell across the bars of the open cage. A shadow cast by a figure dressed in black who was tiptoeing down the dungeon stairs. The figure muttered to himself, cursing as his feet slipped on the mossy stone and he found himself slithering down the remainder of the stairs on his bottom. He arrived at the foot of the stairs, gun clutched in both hands, eyes wide with terror. Staggering to his feet, he blinked in an attempt to see anything in the darkness. "What kind of a place is this?" he asked himself. The echo answered, *This? This? This?*

Shifting his gun into one hand, he fumbled forward, using his other hand to feel along the walls. It wasn't long before his trembling fingers found the granite griffin. As his eyes grew accustomed to the gloom, he could pick out individual features—the flared nostrils, the leonine mane, and the eyeballs frozen in their upward roll.

"The things people keep in their cellars," he remarked,

peering closely at Sab. "Who in their right mind would want to hang on to an ugly brute like you, pal?"

You pal, you pal, you pal, the echo agreed.

Assuming incorrectly that the dungeon offered no threat whatsoever, the hireling tucked his gun in a holster under his armpit and leaned back against the griffin like someone waiting for a passing bus. Furthering this impression of a relaxed commuter, he dangled a cigarette between his lips and rooted in his jacket for a light. He found a single match wedged in the fluff at the bottom of a pocket and searched for a bit of dry stone to strike it on. Reaching upward, he dragged the match across Sab's eyeball. As the match ignited, the griffin appeared to undergo a magical transformation from stone to battered leather. Leather that moved. Leather that reached downward, and with a brief crunch, neatly removed the hireling's head and spat it across the dungeon. The head landed on the floor beside Latch, its severed nerves and sinews causing it to wink in a horribly lifelike fashion.

The remainder crumpled at the knees and pitched forward onto the dungeon floor. The lit match dropped from a lifeless hand and fizzled out on the floor. Latch awoke from a dream into a nightmare. Lifting the newspaper from his face, he found himself eyeball to eyeball with the head of a headless corpse. A trail of blood led to the corpse, which lay leaking gorily under the griffin. Sab looked up at the dungeon ceiling and tried to whistle.

Latch noted that the griffin's mouth was suspiciously red and shiny. Bloody, in fact. "Sab?" Latch's voice came out as a squeak. "What *have* you done?"

The griffin stopped whistling and looked down. "Aaaargh!"

he screamed. "Help! MURDER! Where did *that* come from?" He looked sideways at Latch to see how this was going down. Latch glared at him.

"It's a put-up job!" wailed Sab. "I've been framed! I'm an innocent bystander! How could you believe that I could do such a thing?"

"Because you've got blood running down your chin," Latch said grimly.

"Have I?" Sab patted his mouth. "Oh heck, so I have. . . ."

"*Well?*" said Latch. "What happened?"

"He asked for it," said the griffin, folding his arms and trying to look mean.

"What? He actually said, 'Please, dear griffin, if you're not doing anything too important, could you possibly bite my head off?'" Latch began to lay pages of his newspaper on the floor in an attempt to mop up the blood.

"Well . . . not in so many words," said Sab, avoiding eye contact. "But I knew he was Up to No Good. Check out the gun in his armpit. Really—you'd have done the same yourself."

"Somehow, I very much doubt it," Latch said under his breath. "Stay here. Don't move a muscle. I'm going to find Mrs. McLachlan."

As the sound of his footsteps faded away, Sab stood, as instructed, still as a statue. Leathery hide turned back into stone as the griffin retreated into the state from which he'd been so rudely interrupted. At his feet, the headless gangster resembled a human sacrifice, slain to appease the appetite of an unkind god.

Chilled Attila

Drooling in the kitchen garden, Knot decided that today was his lucky day. He peered through the kitchen window to check that It was really there. First the discovery of Marie Bain's furry slippers discarded by the range, and now this. . . .

In the kitchen, Mrs. McLachlan remonstrated with the malodorous bunny as he tied her to a chair with a length of clothesline. "That knot will never do, dear," she said. "Far too easy to undo. Try a double half-hitch-clove-hangman. Much more secure, don't you think?"

"Shut up," muttered the bunny, adding another granny knot to a chain of knots that dangled like loose knitting from Mrs. McLachlan's hands.

"If you don't mind me saying, *dear*—"

"I *do*. Shut up, would you?"

"It's for your own good, dear. Something your mother forgot to tell you—"

"Shut up, woman, or I'll gag you."

"As I was trying to say, dear, you mustn't shun soap and water. A bath once a day might not be amiss, either. Oh dear, how can I put this without causing offense? Could you not stand quite so close to me, dear, it's just that you . . . smell rather strange."

From the other side of the window, Knot nodded in agreement. Deliciously strange, he thought, rancidly yummy, in fact. With a little whimper of anticipation, the yeti burst into the kitchen, spraying a mist of drool around himself. The rabbit turned round just in time to see the yeti lumbering toward him, arms outstretched.

"WHAT the . . . ?" he screamed as Knot grabbed him with both paws, stuffed him headfirst into his dripping mouth, and poked his thrashing feet in afterward with both thumbs.

"Oh, Knot . . . ," said Mrs. McLachlan sadly. "How could you?"

The yeti gulped apologetically and gazed at Mrs. McLachlan with sorrowful eyes.

"After being so ill this morning, dear. You really should give your tummy time to recover. . . ."

The yeti gave a small belch and tried to look chastened. Mrs. McLachlan wriggled and squirmed in her seat. "We've got a problem at StregaSchloss, Knot," she explained as she flexed and strained at the knotted clothesline. Her feet came undone, closely followed by both hands. "Unwelcome guests. My horoscope was quite right about that, except it isn't lice, it's a particularly vicious kind of rat."

She stood up, the clothesline falling to the floor in coils. "There isn't time to put down poison for this kind of rat, is there?"

The yeti shook his head in what he hoped was an intelligent fashion. He could have turned cartwheels for all the notice Mrs. McLachlan took of him.

"NO," she said, opening her large handbag and rummaging in its depths. "No, Knot, we have to STAMP the vermin out. Eradicate them. Exterminate them. Wipe them off the face of the planet. There's only one thing for it . . ."

Her eyes have gone all funny, Knot thought. Wish I knew what she was on about.

"We need to take them by surprise," continued Mrs. McLachlan. "Can't very well just barge in through the door, can we? They'd hear us coming."

Turning her back on Knot to shield her secret from him, Mrs. McLachlan withdrew a small case from her handbag. I'm really left with no alternative, she decided, unclipping its lid to reveal the keyboard beneath. This situation is outside of my job description, and regrettably I *have* to use all the powers at my disposal to put it to rights. Even if those include the use of magic.

With a grim little smile, she scanned the kitchen for a suitable candidate for the case's transformative powers. Deciding on the upright freezer, she opened its door and propped her case on top of a bag of frozen chicken legs. The exposed keyboard began to frost over. Mrs. McLachlan began to type: F.R.E.E.Z.E.R. Her fingertips left thawed impressions on the frosty keys. Pressing a key named REPLACE, she then typed: S.E.C.R.E.T. P.A.S.S.A.G.E. On a miniature screen on the reverse side of the open lid the prompt appeared: FROM KITCHEN TO WHERE?

Mrs. McLachlan didn't hesitate. Her fingers a blur on the keyboard, she typed: T.O. T.I.T.U.S.'.S. B.E.D.R.O.O.M.

"Please, please, let this not bring the kitchen wall crashing down around our ears," Mrs. McLachlan begged, and holding her breath, she pressed ENTER, snatched her chilly case from the frozen embrace of the chicken legs, and slammed the freezer door shut. There was a muffled explosion, the sound of passages opening up in StregaSchloss where no passages existed before. There was a distant grinding noise and then silence, save for the dripping sound of Knot's drool pattering on the kitchen floor. Hearing the sound of approaching footsteps from the direction of the dungeon, Mrs. McLachlan slipped the case into her pocket and hid in the pantry.

Latch ran into the kitchen, leaving a trail of bloody footprints across the floor. "Mrs. McL . . . Flora," he hissed in a piercing whisper.

Multitudina bolted out of the pantry, followed by Mrs. McLachlan. She stared at the trail of blood behind the butler, took in his startled expression and pale face, and instantly understood.

"You have the look of a man who has just found something exceedingly nasty in the dungeon," she stated.

"Sab beheaded somebody downstairs." Latch shuddered. "It . . . he . . . he had a gun."

"Knot ate the one that was tying me to a chair in the kitchen. He, too, had a gun." Mrs. McLachlan swallowed. "We have a problem."

"Several, I imagine," Latch agreed.

"There's probably more of them and they're undoubtedly armed," said Mrs. McLachlan, stroking the case in her pocket.

"Where are the children?" Latch's voice rose to a shriek.

"That is what we're going to find out," muttered Mrs. McLachlan, opening the freezer door.

Inside, a narrow staircase wound its way upward into darkness. Knot stared after them in some confusion. Why keep a staircase in the freezer? he wondered dimly. And, more to the point, where did the chicken legs go? Also in a state of some confusion, Latch bleated, "Since when was there a secret pass . . . ?" Mrs. McLachlan cut this short by dragging Latch by the hand into the transformed freezer and pushing him ahead of herself, upstairs.

Knot shuffled forward, sniffing Latch's trail of bloody footprints more from habit than appetite. From upstairs came the faint stutter of gunfire. The door to the secret passage was shut firmly in his face.

Something Wicked
This Way Comes

Two rolls of soggy toilet paper later, Pandora decided that she'd cried enough to last her entire lifetime. She quietly opened the bathroom door and sought refuge in her bedroom.

Finding her mother drunk and seeing her brother in tears had completely shattered her belief in her family. Nothing could ever be the same again. They had all been so happy . . . once upon a time.

Hadn't they? Her parents had seemed to love each other, or was that just wishful thinking? Pandora needed reassurance desperately, she needed to see proof positive that there had been happiness, that they had been a family. Then, perhaps, she could find a path back to better times . . . a way to turn the clock back. She hunted along her bookshelves until she found a photograph album that she had shrunk earlier to the size of a thumbnail.

Clumsily leafing through the tiny book, she came across a

recent photograph taken on Damp's first birthday. Peering at the minute picture, she could just about pick out the family group, their pinhead-sized faces gathered round a birthday cake the size of a crumb.

They all looked so small . . . so far away.

They'd been a family then, Pandora thought miserably, observing the microscopic smiles, the air of happiness that permeated the photograph. Two months ago. Only two months and a world can turn itself inside out and upside down. Two months ago, Dad was still around, Damp was just an ordinary-sized baby, and Mrs. McLachlan hadn't moved in. . . . And now . . . this postage-stamp image was all that remained. Dad had gone, Mum was absent due to being drunk, Damp was lost, and Titus . . .

Pandora sighed. Titus, she decided, had lost himself in that blasted computer. When he wasn't playing stupid games on it, he was *thinking* about playing stupid games on it. Pandora stood up. She pulled the last Disposawand from her pocket. A vague plan had begun to take shape in her mind. What if, she wondered with a wild grin flitting across her face, what if I *shrink* the computer? Then Titus won't be able to play on it and he'll have to do something about Dad and Mum and— Pandora's face fell—and Damp. Bother. How do we get Tarantella and Damp back if the computer's the size of a matchbox? Bother, bother. . . . Absently sucking the end of her wand, Pandora opened her bedroom door and sleepwalked out into the corridor, her mind full of a plan.

There *must* be a way to do this, she reasoned as she walked slowly toward Titus's room. There *has* to be a way . . . shrink the computer, but YES! That's IT! Keep the modem and the

CD-ROM the same size. YES, YES, YES, what a *brain*, Pandora, what a *star*, what a child *prodigy*. Pandora was so captivated by her own brilliance that she was through the door of Titus's bedroom before she realized that he had a visitor. On reflection, she thought, *not* a visitor—an intruder.

Titus's eyes met hers. In his gaze, Pandora read fear, pain, and utter misery. Without thinking, she raised her left hand and began to draw lazy circles in the air with her wand.

"Right, kid," Pronto said, waving his gun. "Over here. Don't make a squeak or your brother's a human colander."

"He means it," muttered Titus. "Just do as he says, Pan."

Pandora advanced on Pronto, her wand poised to cast the spell.

"And put that stick down," added Pronto. "It's making me nervous."

"This old thing?" Pandora said innocently, gazing at the wand as if she'd just noticed it. "Here—catch!"

Titus flinched and braced himself. The wand flew through the air toward Pronto, who was completely taken aback. Reflexively he thrust out his gun to knock the wand out of the air. The wand and the gun made contact. There was a dazzling flash. Titus and Pandora reeled backward, their frazzled eyeballs temporarily out of order as afterimages of intense light seared their retinas. Blinking frantically, Pandora was first to sense that everything had not gone according to plan. Contrary to what she'd imagined when she cast her spell, Pronto was *not* holding a miniaturized firearm, capable only of immobilizing ladybugs and bruising crane flies.

Pronto gazed at his outstretched arm, a nasty grin stretching across his face. He no longer held a small machine gun. Instead, Pronto was stroking the oily barrel of the deadliest automatic weapon known to man. So sophisticated, it didn't have a trigger, it picked up signals from the user's brain. So advanced, it didn't have a telescopic sight, it had an infrared flesh-detector to locate and lock on to its target. Such a deadly weapon that its inventor had turned it on himself in a fit of remorse for having created such a lethal artifact. Its name was Wormwood and it lay hissing quietly in Pronto's arms, its blind snout jerking from side to side as it located first Pandora and then Titus.

"Oh, well DONE," Titus said bitterly. "What a GENIUS. What a STAR you are, sister dear."

Pandora rubbed her eyes and glared at her brother. "It's that wand," she wailed. "I did everything right, but the *wand* didn't work."

"This old thing?" Pronto purred, picking up the fallen wand and examining it. "'Contrawand,'" he read, "'reverses spells, undoes charms, and nixes hexes.' Hang on, there's something else in very small letters. 'The manufacturers recommend six uses only before safe disposal as hazardous magical waste.'"

Pandora's shoulders slumped.

"Well . . . ?" demanded Titus.

"Actually," admitted Pandora, "the wand worked perfectly."

"I'll second *that*," gloated Pronto, patting Wormwood. From the gun came a ghastly sound like forks being dragged across a plate.

The children shuddered.

"Right," Pronto continued, addressing Titus, "where were we before we were so *charmingly* interrupted? Ah yes, UP AGAINST THE WALL AND SAY YOUR GOODBYES."

A Pound of Flesh

on Lucifer di S'Embowelli Borgia gazed at his reflection in the mirror. Dressed in a lilac hospital gown with a disposable paper hat covering his skull, he was aware that he did not look his best. This impression was supported by the fact that his vast nose was covered in blue lines and words like "nip," "tuck," "slash," and "tear along the dotted line." These scrawled instructions together with the grid of blue lines made the Don's nose resemble a street map drawn in haste on the back of a napkin. Very undignified, the Don thought, but it will all be worth it. Today I go under the knife of Italy's top plastic surgeon, Professore Flense-Filleto. Not only will he sculpt me the perfect nose but he and his team of doctors and nurses will provide me with the perfect alibi. The Don permitted himself the tiniest of smiles, imagining that evening's newspaper reports:

Don Knifed
While Brother Crisped

Don Lucifer di S'Embowelli Borgia was undergoing surgery in an exclusive Milanese hospital while a mysterious fire broke out at his secluded palazzo. Firemen called to the scene arrived too late to rescue the Don's beloved brother, Luciano, from the inferno that razed the palazzo to the ground.

Police sources reveal that the Don is not under suspicion.

Don Lucifer bared his teeth in a feral grin. Perfect. With all witnesses able to swear that on the day of the "accident," the main suspect had booked himself into their hospital for a major rhinoplasty, there was little that the police could do to pin the "mysterious fire" on him. Perfect. A master plan, in fact.

There was a discreet knock at the door. The Don leapt across the room and arranged himself on the bed. Professore Flense-Filleto swung into the room, followed by a posse of young doctors and nurses.

"We're ready for you now, Signor di S'Embowelli Borgia," said the professore. "All the knives are razor sharp and I've been practicing my sewing on an old bit of chamois leather, har-dee-har, fnaar-fnaar."

Obediently, the posse broke out in forced laughter. The Don paled. Propelled by three nurses, his bed began to move slowly across the room.

Opening the door, the professore oozed confidence. "Not nervous, are we? Mustn't mind my little jokes. We've got a lovely little elephant's trunk just waiting for you in the operating room, haven't we, nurse? Haar-haar, fnaar."

Wearily, the posse sniggered on cue. The Don sat bolt upright in bed. Pushing him back into a horizontal position, the professore continued. "Nothing can possibly go wrong, signor. We have technology at our fingertips. We'll hook you up to our machines, everything computer-controlled and linked to several hospitals across the world, and *that* way we have the skills of many of the finest surgeons at our disposal. You could say that you are on the cutting edge of science, hurr-hurr-hurr."

The nurses gave the Don's bed a particularly vicious push, and he found himself barreling through the doors to the operating room.

"Just a little jab and you'll soon drift away," one of the nurses said, bending over the bed and slipping a needle into the Don's arm. She straightened up and began sorting scalpels and forceps. "Count backward from ten for me, Signor di S'Embowelli Borgia . . . ?"

Obediently, the Don began, "Ten, nine, eight, seven lawyers, six . . . six policemen, five alive, alive oh, four no more, four sharksss . . . Ragu . . . Lucianoooo . . ."

His eyeballs slid backward in his head. The Don's last awareness was of straps being placed round his head and arms, and the disembodied voice of the professore saying, "Signor, is that a fine pair of sunglasses you're wearing or are those your nostrils? Huurr-hurr, dee-fnaar."

You're Toast

Signor Strega-Borgia clapped a hand to his forehead. This computer infestation was beyond him. He had spent the better part of a working day frantically dismantling computer mainframes, and still the rats eluded him. No sooner would he undo the maintenance panels on one monitor than the rats would disappear from within it with a squeak. Within seconds, they would reappear on a nearby screen with their pink noses pressed up against the glass in a demented form of peekaboo.

To add to his discomfort, the temperature in the computer room was climbing rapidly. Signor Strega-Borgia loosened his tie, removed his jacket, and rolled up his shirt sleeves. After a moment, he removed his shoes and socks. The marble floor felt warm underfoot.

"Strange . . . ," he muttered, padding across the room to a working terminal. He keyed in **stregaschloss.co.uk** and stopped. In front of him the cursor blinked, on, off, on, off. If only it was all so simple, he thought, on, off, yes, no. Despite their apparent complexity, computers work on a binary system of choices. On or off were the only options. No in-between choices. No shades of gray. Just two choices. And what if you make the wrong choice, he thought, like that awful day when I stormed out of StregaSchloss, fueled by a moment's rage. . . .

The empty screen waited. Taking a deep draft from a bottle of warm Coke, Signor Strega-Borgia began feverishly to type an e-mail to his son. After a few paragraphs, he found that the sweat trickling down his forehead was stinging his eyes. His shirt stuck to his back and his fingers slithered around on sweaty keys. "Need some air in here," he muttered, heading for the door.

PUSH, it read. Signor Strega-Borgia pushed. Nothing happened. Signor Strega-Borgia pushed again. The door remained firmly shut. Signor Strega-Borgia hurled his weight against the door. Still, nothing. Taking several paces backward, he ran at the door and launched a flying kick at it.

He slowly picked himself up off the floor, checked that no major limbs were broken, and crawled to the door. Pressing his eye up to the keyhole, Signor Strega-Borgia singed his eyelashes on the metal. Disbelieving the evidence of his eyelashes, he felt the keyhole with his hand. "OUCH!" he yelled. The metal was red-hot.

It was at this point that Luciano Strega-Borgia gave up hope of ever seeing his family again.

Stripped down to his boxer shorts, Signor Strega-Borgia sat panting at a computer terminal. The temperature in the computer room rose by the minute. Half an hour before, it had been perfect for cooking meringues; now it was the ideal temperature to roast turkey. Large turkeys.

Two tears tracked down his cheeks, evaporating as they slid chinward. Signor Strega-Borgia was typing what he knew to be his last letter. He paused to wipe his sweat-slippery hands on his discarded shirt. Blinking through his tears, he looked at his words on the screen in front of him:

> Dearest Titus, beloved Pandora, adored Damp, and my beautiful wife,

Recalling their faces, he tried not to imagine them held at gunpoint, pale and terrified, his beloved family at the mercy of Pronto. It will be all right, he reassured himself, Lucifer has what he wants and he will call off his hired thugs. Hoping against hope that this was indeed the case, he returned to his e-mail and typed:

> I shall shortly be leaving you forever, but before i go, I want to say these few words . . .

> Titus—my son, my firstborn. I loved you from the moment I heard your newborn wail. as I watched you grow from an infant into a fine young man, my love grew daily. be brave, my son, be true.

Signor Strega-Borgia paused to blow his nose loudly into his shirt. Stifling a sob, he continued:

> and there's a keyboard shortcut for Death & Destruction II that neutralizes the force field round Nettlefold. It's control, shift, alt while your left hand holds down option, shift, caps lock. good hunting!

Pandora—my darling girl, my eldest daughter. born with the August moon flooding your eyes, you have brought perpetual summer into my life. Your regal dignity surrounded you since you were a tiny baby, my princess. be brave, my love, and remember—at least this way, I won't embarrass you when you grow up.

One last thing—no pierced ears, noses, or whatever until you're at least 21, and that's final.

and Damp—my little baby, my sweetest flower. by the time you are old enough to read this yourself, you won't remember me at all.

He paused again, struck by the thought that for his youngest child he would be nothing. Not even a vague memory. A blank dada. The thought was not a happy one. The soles of his feet began to feel uncomfortably hot, so perched on a melting stool, he carried on.

You'll have to ask your mama about me. ask her about raspberries blown on your tummy, about how we laughed together, about how much I loved you.

May your life be full of flowers, love, and laughter. and know this—that your daddy loved you to bits.

He stopped for a short weep. The winking cursor blinked on and off, waiting mindlessly for more words. "It's so *sad*," howled Signor Strega-Borgia. "I won't see any of them grow up. I'll be a blackened crisp while they slowly forget me. . . ."

He picked up his shirt, noticing that despite having used it as a giant handkerchief, it was dry . . . and very hot. Blowing his nose yet again, he came to the final part of his farewell letter.

My love, my life, my dearest only wife . . .

He typed frantically for as long as he could, stopping occasionally to pour warm Coke over his head in a hopeless attempt to cool himself down. Finally he reached the end of the letter. Sniffing, he typed in the address:

my best-loved family@stregaschloss.co.uk

and blowing a kiss to the screen, he pressed ENT and ER. To his relief, up on the screen came the reassuring words: MESSAGE SENT.

Emptying the last drops of Coke over his head, Signor Strega-Borgia sat and waited for death.

The Music of the Pipes

Pronto's arms ached with the weight of the gun Wormwood. "Come *on*," he groaned. "How long does it take to say goodbye?"

"A long time if you're a Strega-Borgia," muttered Pandora.

"You see, we have to say it in Urdu, Serbo-Croatian, Mandarin . . . ," explained Titus.

"Not to mention Xhosa, Pig Latin, ancient Greek, and Yibble," added Pandora.

"Two minutes more," warned Pronto, drumming his fingers on Wormwood's barrel. "Don't think I don't know when I'm having the Michelangelo taken."

"Ot-whay ow-nay?" whispered Titus.

"On't-day o-knay," said his sister, nibbling the skin round her gnawed fingernails. "E're-way oomed-day." She was trying not to look at Wormwood. In her terror, her eyes scanned round Titus's room, finally alighting on a gloomy oil painting that had hung in the bedroom for as long as she could remember. It was a particularly hideous depiction of a fox cornered by men in red jackets and fat, drooling hounds. The fox, as could be expected, was looking rather nervous, the hounds somewhat hungry, and the red-jacketed men faintly nauseous. The whole had been painted in somber earth colors of mud, sludge, and silage, and titled *The Unspeakable in Pursuit of the Inedible*.

It hung on the wall, just behind Pronto, massive and ugly . . . and ever so slightly askew. In fact, not askew, Pandora realized. It looked just like a vast door, slightly ajar. . . .

At the top of the secret stairway, Latch and Mrs. McLachlan halted. Trying not to sneeze in the dusty air, they whispered to each other in the darkness.

"We'll surprise him," hissed Latch. "I'll burst in, tackle him, hurl him to the ground, get his arms up behind his back, kick his gun to one side, frog-march him downstairs, and phone the police. . . ."

"Er, no, dear, I *don't* think so," whispered Mrs. McLachlan, discreetly removing her little case from her pocket and flipping it open. "Too risky—we can't have stray bullets flying around."

Attempting to shield the case from Latch's inquiring gaze, she switched it on and peered within. It lit up with a silvery glow, illuminating her face and causing Latch to wonder why, at a time like this, his companion had decided to turn girly and powder her nose.

"Have you a better suggestion?" he muttered through clenched teeth. "For heaven's sake, woman, there isn't time to gaze in your mirror, come *on*!" And without waiting for a reply, he burst through the secret door into Titus's bedroom.

★ ★ ★

Later, Pandora would recall that everything moved very quickly from the moment that she'd noticed the off-kilter painting. One minute she was wondering why it appeared to hang from the wall on hinges, and next thing, Latch was flying through it like a . . . well, really, like a *hero*, she admitted as Latch landed on top of that vile gangster with the horrible gun.

"BANZAIIIIiii!" yelled Latch, launching himself at Pronto. "GERRRRONIMO!" he added for effect as he knocked Wormwood out of Pronto's grasp.

Pronto was scrabbling across the floor in pursuit of Wormwood, followed by Latch, who was intent on fastening his hands around the thug's throat, when Mrs. McLachlan stepped through the hole in the wall with a dazzling object held in her outstretched hands. A beam of light streamed from it, bathing Pronto in a silver glow.

The gangster flailed and screamed, and Latch, sensing victory, fastened his hands around Pronto's neck.

"Oh, for goodness' sake!" wailed Mrs. McLachlan as she saw what a ghastly mistake she had made. "What a *stupid* idiot. What a *moron*. What a cretinous act of cybermagic. What a dumb thing to do!"

"WHAT?" roared Latch, his hands tight round Pronto's throat. "What have I done *now*, woman?" From beneath him came a ghastly sound like a strangulated wheeze.

"Not you, dear, *me*. I missed. My aim was off." Mrs. McLachlan tutted, closing her case with a snap and instantly dropping it into her pocket. She crossed the room to where Wormwood lay twitching and spinning on the floor. "This," she explained, picking up the gun with some difficulty, "*this* was my intended target."

The gun hissed in her arms, twitching this way and that, seeking skin. "Revolting thing," said Mrs. McLachlan, reaching under the trigger for the on/off switch. Immediately, Wormwood slumped over her arm, floppy as a disk and pliable as a Slinky.

Latch gazed at her in some confusion. If the gun hadn't become her target, what had? A snort from Titus caused him to turn back to his wheezing victim.

"Oh, Latch," gasped Pandora, "if you could only see your face!" Bewildered, Latch slowly released his grip on the fallen Pronto.

A strangely familiar droning groan came from beneath the butler's kilt. Titus and Pandora made eye contact and burst into hysterical giggles. In a forlorn attempt at maintaining some shred of dignity, Latch rose to his feet, dusted down his kilt, and cleared his throat. "Would someone be kind enough to explain to me why I find myself locked in mortal combat with that . . . that *thing*?" he spluttered, pointing at what lay on the floor at his feet.

Pronto had undergone a magical transformation. Where seconds before he had stood, exuding bristling Mafia menace, now he lay metamorphosed into a giant set of bagpipes, droning like a stale tartan fart.

Titus prodded the ex-thug with his toe. Pronto obliged with a desolate wheeze.

Trying her hardest to keep a serious expression pinned to her face, Mrs. McLachlan wrapped an arm round Latch's shoulder and began to explain what had really happened. "You see, you were just a wee bitty impetuous, dear. If you'd waited for me, I could have turned that nasty gun into . . ."

Seeing the look on Latch's face, Mrs. McLachlan hastily changed tack. "Now, dear, if you hadn't been so brave and rushed in to tackle that brute single-handed . . . ," she crooned.

A tiny smile began to hover round Latch's mouth.

". . . and with no thought for your own personal safety . . . ," Mrs. McLachlan sighed admiringly.

Bored with all this Latch flattery, Titus drifted back to his computer screen and discovered that it was now working again. To his delight, there was a message informing him that he had mail. Titus downloaded it and began to read while Pandora experimented with the musical possibilities of a metamorphosed thug.

". . . and the way you dropped him with just one blow—I'm just lost in admiration . . . ," murmured Mrs. McLachlan in the background.

Pandora leaned over her brother's shoulder to read whatever it was that he was so engrossed in.

". . . such strong hands you have, and you cut a fine figure in a kilt . . ." Somehow Mrs. McLachlan was keeping a straight face as she laid the flattery on with a shovel.

"OH NO!" wailed Titus. "DAD! NO! Help, we've got to do SOMETHING!"

"Somebody get Mum!" yelled Pandora. "Something awful's about to happen! LATCH! GET MUM! NOW!"

Inside Titus's modem, Tarantella sighed: There they go again, she thought. One drama after another. And so much noise and fuss. She looked down at the sleeping Damp. The baby was oblivious to her siblings' recent near-extinction, her father's imminent crispdom, and her mother's inebriation. She slept, slung in the cradle of Tarantella's eight legs, cocooned in spider silk, her mouth slightly open and her cheeks flushed pink from the warmth of the modem's internal workings.

The Revenge of the Hot Toddy

Signora Strega-Borgia proved difficult to wake. "S'amatter?" she protested as Latch hauled her out of bed and Mrs. McLachlan dragged her under a cold shower. "Wossarush? S'apanic? Aargh! STOP! It's *freezing*! Wossgoinon? Aah! No! STOP THIS!"

Mrs. McLachlan, satisfied that her employer was now fully awake, turned off the shower. Signora Strega-Borgia lurched out of the bathroom leaving a trail of wet footprints behind her. The nanny followed, holding out a bath towel by way of a peace offering.

"This had better be good, Mrs. McLachlan," Signora Strega-Borgia said, ignoring the towel and pulling a bathrobe around herself. "There had better be a *very* good reason for knocking me out with your fiendish hot toddy, *then* trying to drown me in that—"

Mrs. McLachlan interrupted, "Madam, hurry, it's the Master and the wee baby. . . ." Her voice broke.

"What is it? Where's Damp? Luciano? Flora, *tell* me. Are they hurt? Injured?" Signora Strega-Borgia's eyes filled. "Oh *no*. Not dead, *no*! Tell me not. TELL ME THEY'RE NOT DEAD, Flora. FLORA!"

"No, madam, but . . ."

"Where *are* they?" screamed Signora Strega-Borgia, grabbing Mrs. McLachlan's shoulders and shaking her. "Where ARE they?"

"Oh, madam," Mrs. McLachlan sobbed, "they're in the computer."

"I don't *believe* it!" yelled Signora Strega-Borgia, abruptly releasing Mrs. McLachlan's shoulders and pacing round her bedroom, addressing the furniture. "She drags me out of my sickbed, half-drowns me in water cold enough to give a polar bear hypothermia, leads me to believe that my baby daughter and missing husband are in mortal danger, and for what? FOR WHAT?" She paused in front of her reflection in the dressing table mirror. "FOR WHAT?" she bawled.

The mirror rippled and spoke:

> *Thou art the fairest,*
> *as everyone knows,*
> *but thou hast ice water*
> *dripping off thy nose . . .*

"Shut UP!" yelled Signora Strega-Borgia, continuing through clenched teeth. "For what, I ask you? Woken, drowned, *and* frozen in order to learn that baby and spouse are on the computer. How earth-shattering. How desperately important. How—"

"Madam," interrupted Mrs. McLachlan.

"Yes, MRS. McLachlan?" said Signora Strega-Borgia, in a

voice that dripped vitriol. "What now? Perhaps you need to tell me that . . . let me see . . . it's Saturday? The earth is still turning? Night will follow day?"

Showing remarkable patience in the face of Signora Strega-Borgia's tide of sarcasm, Mrs. McLachlan continued, speaking slowly and clearly as if to a small child. "I said *IN*, madam, not *on*. *IN*, as in, 'Your husband and daughter are *in* the computer.'"

"*What?*" wailed Signora Strega-Borgia. "No, don't answer. Show me. Please. I don't care *how* they got in there, just take me to them."

A Muffin-Scented Gale

"Titus, can you send an e-mail to Dad?"

"Fat lot of good that would do," said Titus, his eyes glued to his father's last message on the screen. "E-mail's not going to save him now."

"Titus! Yes or no? Can we e-mail him?"

"Yes," sniffed Titus. "We can. Now. Since the computer seems to be working again. Why? What's the point? What are you doing, Pandora?"

Pandora looked up from where she'd been hunting under her brother's bed. "Got it."

"Got what?"

"The wand, Titus. I've got an idea. I'll shrink myself like Damp, and you blow me into the modem, e-mail me to Dad, I'll shrink *him*, and—"

"Oh BRILLIANT!" yelled Titus. "Oh, Pan, what a GREAT PLAN! What a STAR! You're a GENIUS!"

"Yes, I have to agree," said Pandora, circling the wand round and round her body.

"WAIT!" screamed Titus, grabbing her wrist. "Stand on the modem, or on the table. If you shrink on the floor, I'll never find you."

"Oops. Good thinking, Titus." Pandora clambered onto the table and began again. She spun with the wand, slowly at first, and then faster and faster until, with a final thrust, she pointed the wand directly at her heart. "Oh no . . . ," she wailed.

With a crash, the table beneath her gave way.

"Oh NO," groaned Titus. "You forgot, didn't you, dumbo?"

"Contrawand," moaned Pandora, her gigantic mouth pressed against the plaster cornice of Titus's bedroom ceiling. "Hang on a tick. . . ."

Pandora filled the room.

Her massive feet pressed hard against the bedroom door, her mountainous bottom swamped Titus's bed, and with one colossal fist, she plucked her brother off his seat and brought him within range.

"Who're you calling 'dumbo'?" she said.

Titus, gazing into an eyeball the size of a watermelon, swallowed painfully. "N-n-not you, sister dear."

"I thought not," Pandora sighed. "Listen, squirt, much as I'd love to play around with you, we don't have the time, so if you'll be good enough to pass me my wand from under that table. . . ."

She gently placed her brother back on the floor and he passed her the wand. In her wardrobe-sized hand, it looked like a matchstick as she made dainty circles round her stomach.

"Careful," warned Titus. "Any bigger and you'll go through the roof."

With a patter of falling plaster, Pandora resumed her normal size.

"*Right,*" she said, spitting out bits of ceiling. "Let's put the modem on this footstool, and I'll climb up here, and . . ."

Round and round, she spun the wand, and with a grin for Titus . . . vanished.

"Pan? PANDORA? Oh NO! Now what?" He bent over the footstool, trying hard not to breathe. "Pandora—yell if you're still here." He leaned closer to where he hoped his shrunken sister might be, his ear close to the modem.

A tiny voice said, "Yeuchhh. Don't you ever wash in there? You're so GROSS, Titus."

"Get ready, Pandora. Curl up in a ball, and that way you might not break too many limbs . . . five, four." Titus leaned carefully over the footstool and stood, fingers poised over the keyboard. He took a deep breath.

"I'm scared, Titus."

"Three, two, don't be a wuss, Pan, one . . . PUFF! We have liftoff. . . ."

There was no applause, no spectacular blast of smoke. There was just a profound absence of Pandora.

There was a huge muffin-scented gale, sweeping her up, tumbling her over and over. There were spinning colors, a kaleidoscopic whirlpool, and then . . . black. There was pain all over as she crashed and bumped into unknown things in the modem. But mainly, there was fear. Something breathed in there. More than one thing, in fact.

Pandora had never felt so afraid in her life. What if . . . ? No, don't. Titus called me a wuss. Titus doesn't know the half of it.

Give me a couple of lengths with Tock any day. Pull yourself together, girl, somewhere out there are your father, your baby sister, and your favorite spi—

"TaranTELLA!" shrieked Pandora.

"ShhhHH! *Quiet,*" hissed the spider, clamping a hairy leg over Pandora's mouth. "You'll wake the baby, and *believe* me, you don't want to do that." Tarantella shuddered and released Pandora. "Who ever would have thought that such a hairless little wrinkly could make such a din."

"Oh, Tarantella, well DONE. You *found* her." Pandora reached out to stroke Damp's face and stumbled. In front of her, a black void opened up.

"Whoa. Careful," warned Tarantella, snatching Pandora back to safety. "Fall into that and you could end up *anywhere,*" she said, opening her eyes wide for emphasis. *"Anywhere."*

Above their heads, blue flashes of electricity crackled. Each flash illuminated the industrial landscape that surrounded them. Giant lentils on spindly legs alternated with vast stripy cylinders poised on metal scaffolds. Towering skyscrapers perched on a landscape crosshatched with gleaming metal runways. It was bleak, it was ugly, and it was utterly devoid of life.

"Where is this?" whispered Pandora.

"This is the printed circuit board," intoned Tarantella, dropping her voice to a whisper and adding, "that black tunnel into which you so nearly fell, that . . . that is the void, the portal."

Pandora peered at the spider in the gloom. Tarantella's eyes glowed.

"That's the way in, d'you mean?"

"Dear child, think of it as an entry ramp leading onto a great motorway . . . or perhaps a trickling brook that turns into a great river and eventually rushes into the sea . . . or perhaps—"

"Tarantella," interrupted Pandora, "how do I hitch a lift on an outgoing e-mail?"

"You simply stand in front of one, just like you'd stand in front of a speeding tractor-trailer. *Just* like, believe me. Hits you like a ten-ton truck, whizzes you off into the Web, and seconds later, SPLAT, you've arrived." Seeing Pandora's horrified expression, Tarantella expanded further. "I imagine it's similar to what flies feel when they're spread across a windshield. One minute buzz, buzz . . . and the next thing that goes through their minds is their bottom."

Pandora groaned. Her Rescue Dad Plan appeared to have a serious drawback. But, she thought, hang on a minute. . . . "How come you're not dead? And Damp? You're not both windshield smears, are you?"

Tarantella arranged herself for a cozy chat. "What you've failed to grasp, O leggily challenged one, is that this is *virtual* travel. Not *real* travel. *Not* the same thing at all."

Oh heck, thought Pandora. Do NOT Pass Go until the spider has delivered an interminable lecture. . . .

"Look, hairless one, when you send an e-mail, you're not sending a bit of paper with a letter written on it, are you?"

"No . . . but," said Pandora, propping her chin on her knees and trying to look interested.

"Nor does your e-mail travel only on cables and wires, does it?"

"Nhuh?" said Pandora, beginning to lose the plot.

"Sometimes it's bounced through space via satellite, or zapped out by microwave . . ."

"Duh," agreed Pandora. It was warm in the modem. Warm and cozy. She leaned back into Tarantella's furry body and watched Damp's eyes roll behind her eyelids.

". . . so you see it's utterly painless," droned the spider. "If you don't believe me, I'll show you."

In the vast spaces beyond the confines of the modem, Titus brought his fingers thudding down on the keyboard. Spotting an opportunity to demonstrate the wonders of Web travel, Tarantella acted swiftly. "Look, here comes one now. Hang on tight. . . ."

Holding Pandora and Damp snug against her abdomen, Tarantella leapt in front of Titus's outgoing message to `dad@mafia.org.ital`.

Endgame

Death was horribly slow in coming, thought Signor Strega-Borgia. The air in the computer room stank of melting plastic as one by one the banks of computers surrounding him overheated, sent out onscreen warnings of system errors, and, with small puffs of black smoke, went down.

This must be what lobsters feel like as they boil alive, he thought. Droplets of sweat dripped off his nose and hissed as they landed on the floor. The air burned his throat with each breath he took. Forget lobsters, he thought, more like barbe-cued chicken. To distract himself from his imminent extinction, Signor Strega-Borgia loaded *Revenge IV* into the last working computer. He huddled on a chair, curled in a ball, waiting for the game to run.

Onscreen came a menu: CHOOSE YOUR WEAPON.

nuclear warhead

nail-studded club
rusty dagger
vial of vitriol
box of dynamite

"Oh very good," groaned Signor Strega-Borgia as the last choice scrolled past him: flamethrower.

He armed himself and clicked onto the main menu:

battleground, choose from the following:
- ❏ supermarket on a saturday afternoon
- ❏ london taxi stand at 11:20 p.m. on a rainy friday night
- ❏ the oval office, washington, d.c.
- ❏ phning ptui jungle, somewhere in the subtropics

Signor Strega-Borgia sighed. For some reason, this game was failing to hold his attention. He gazed blankly at the screen, where little figures armed with nail-studded clubs were invading the fish counter in a busy supermarket. A message box appeared: YOU HAVE MAIL.

Signor Strega-Borgia stared at the message. He wondered who on earth it was from as his fingers slid across the keyboard. He found the Open Mail command and pressed ENT and ER. Maybe he could ask for help. Maybe it was the local fire station e-mailing the palazzo, to inquire why it was belching smoke and flames all over the rural Italian countryside. Maybe it was one of his evil half brother's associates, checking that he'd melted. He glared at the screen, willing it to hurry up and download this unknown message. Another box appeared on-screen:

"*What* message?" wailed Signor Strega-Borgia. "There's nothing there. It's empty. It's BLANK!"

Over the crackle and hiss of the encroaching inferno came a tiny squeaking sound. "*Not* the rats," moaned Signor Strega-Borgia. "Burned to a crisp in the company of several roasted rodents is *not* a nice way to go."

The Internet journey to the palazzo was swift and brutal. Pandora's eyelids were dragged back into her skull and her eyes streamed. It was *exactly* like being a bug stuck to the windshield of a speeding tractor-trailer. Space whooshed past her, deafening, blinding, and utterly terrifying. In the midst of the technological maelstrom, she caught a brief flash of something strangely familiar. . . . Several somethings, in fact.

Heading on a collision course toward Tarantella, Damp, and Pandora were the missing rat babies, their yellow teeth bared in the airflow, their tails streaming out behind them. Just as it seemed inevitable that the two parties of e-travelers should collide, the ratlets veered off to the left and vanished. Almost immediately, with an excruciatingly jarring impact, Pandora, Damp, and Tarantella arrived at the portal. The spider nimbly dragged her cargo onto a ledge, from where they could look down in safety onto the endless rush of traffic below.

"*There*," said Tarantella, "now you know. Just give me a minute to powder my nose and I'll take you back home."

"Where are we now?" groaned Pandora, checking herself for breakages.

"Does it matter?" said the spider, producing a tiny mirror

from a hidden pouch and peering at her reflection. "Let's return this baby to where she belongs *before* she wakes up. . . ."

"I can't go back yet," whispered Pandora. "I have to find Dad."

"You've lost your father?" Tarantella muttered through a mouthful of lipstick. She puckered up at her reflection with a kissing sound and continued, "How very careless of you. . . . I ate mine."

Pandora shuddered. "Where's the way out?" she said.

"Up thataway," said the spider, indicating a steep tunnel leading away from their ledge.

Pandora stood up and hugged Tarantella. "Awwwk. My lipstick . . . ," moaned the spider. "What was *that* for?"

"Look after Damp till I return," said Pandora, "and if I'm not back in twenty minutes, go home without me."

"Now hang *on* a minute," the spider said, her eyes growing saucer-like with alarm. "You're *not* leaving me with this baby. No *way*. It might leak, it might smell, it might . . . WAKE UP AGAIN. No, no, NO. Wherever you go, I'll be right behind you."

"I hoped you'd say that." Pandora smirked. "Come on, then, this way."

Together they scrabbled up the tunnel toward the light. Tarantella pushed Pandora onward when the tunnel climbed steeply. Damp rocked from side to side, swaying under the spider's abdomen, rocked in a hairy cradle.

"It's getting hotter," Pandora said, stating the obvious. The sides of the tunnel were no longer hard and cool. Each step they took sank into warm rubbery stickiness. "It's like wading through molasses," she moaned.

"Nearly there," gasped Tarantella.

At last they arrived in a challenged version of the modem at StregaSchloss. Puddles of plastic oozed from the ceiling, melting giant lentils swayed on red-hot legs, giant wires glowed white beneath their feet, and they ran in the direction of the light.

The squeaking grew louder. Signor Strega-Borgia slumped in front of the screen. To the smell of melting plastic would soon be added the odor of crispy rat. It was unbearable. He buried his face in his hands and wept.

Through his tears, he saw something tiny move by the modem. Something small, growing bigger . . . and bigger . . . and bigger . . . with each blink of his unbelieving eyes. It yelled. It wailed. It groaned. "DAD!"

"Bwaaaaaaa . . ."

"Oh Lord, here we go again, pat pat, rock rock, soothe, pat."

"PanDORA!" screamed Signor Strega-Borgia, automatically brushing the spider off his desk. "DAMP!"

"Don't mind me," muttered Tarantella, "I'm just the substitute nanny. What's the odd broken leg when one has so many. . . . OUCH! This floor's *roasting!*"

She sprang onto an unmelted chair and glared at the tender reunion taking place in front of her.

"Oh, DAD."

"Oh, DARLINGS, oh, my little *girls,* Pandora, Damp."

Not so little, Pandora thought with relief. In fact, normal size, thank heavens.

"Great," said the spider, "now that we've established who we all are, can we leave? Please? I, for one, am not equipped for such a heat wave."

"We have to get *out* of here," said Pandora, looking doubtfully at her wand.

Tarantella began a slow handclap.

Six uses only, it had said. In a panic, Pandora counted: One—Pronto/Wormwood, Two—herself (huge), three—herself (normal), four—herself (microscopic), five—Damp, Tarantella, and herself (normal). She needed to use it two more times. Once to shrink them all for the journey home, and one last time to return them to life-sized once they arrived safely at StregaSchloss. That made seven. She bit her lip and decided.

"We have to risk it. Hold Damp, grab on to me, and . . ."

Tarantella jumped into Pandora's arms. Signor Strega-Borgia grabbed Damp. The door to the computer room burst into flames.

"QUICK!" screamed Pandora. "Hold on TIGHT!"

She spun the wand, round and round, faster and faster. Damp opened her mouth wide and screamed. Blinding smoke poured into the room. Tarantella choked and spluttered, and in her panic, wrapped all eight of her legs tightly round Pandora's nose.

Faster and faster. In the computer room, the lights flickered and went out.

"RUN!" yelled Pandora.

Coughing and sobbing, they waded through the melting modem, fell down the tunnel and out onto the ledge. With a final howl from the terrified Damp, they threw themselves off the ledge, and fell screaming, down into the stream of traffic.

A Bit of a Mix-up

Signora Strega-Borgia sat chewing her fingernails, peering at the screen on Titus's computer. For the tenth time, she asked, "How long *now*? D'you think they'll be all right? Can't you send me too?"

Titus groaned.

"I can't stand this. Waiting, just waiting. Doing nothing. It's unbearable. . . ." She trailed off, hiccuped twice, and devoured another fingernail. Mrs. McLachlan silently refilled her employer's coffee cup.

Across the room, Latch tied a final knot in the rope binding the transformed Pronto. "And *that*'ll put a bend in your chanter," he muttered to his captive.

Signora Strega-Borgia wiped her nose on her sleeve and began again. "Titus? How long now? D'you think—"

"*MUM!*"

"Sorry. I just can't stand this. . . ." She gulped another mouthful of coffee.

"Yes. You've told me. Ten times. Waiting. Just waiting. Doing nothing."

"Titus, just because you *once* found me rolling around in a hot toddy–induced stupor, doesn't mean that you can treat me like an imbecile for the rest of time. . . ."

Titus glared at his mother.

"It was a *mistake*, Titus. People make mistakes. Your father and I made a mistake when we split up. Mrs. McLachlan made a mistake and turned that . . . that creature into a set of bagpipes. . . ."

"Sab made a mistake," added Latch helpfully.

Mrs. McLachlan glared at him. Not *now*, she mouthed.

"Um, er, no, he didn't," amended Latch. "*I'm* mistaken."

"I made a mistake," admitted Titus. "I sneezed my baby sister into the modem and sent her . . . sent her . . ." He burst into tears.

"Oh, Titus." Signora Strega-Borgia wrapped her arms round her son's shaking shoulders. "Oh, my dear, it was all a big mistake. . . . What's *that*?"

"What?" sniffed Titus.

"On your computer television thingy." She flapped vaguely at the screen. YOU HAVE MAIL.

"Pandora!" yelled Titus. "She's *BACK*!" His fingers flew over the keys, downloading the incoming mail and opening it as far as he could. "Stand back," he warned. "Don't *breathe*."

Signora Strega-Borgia sneezed carefully over her left shoulder. A large gobbet of goo flew across the room and landed on the fallen Pronto.

"Perfect," said Latch, with deep satisfaction.

"Oh *my*," breathed Titus, backing away from the footstool on which the modem sat. "Oh *MY*."

Appearing in front of him was an odd assortment of tiny shapes.

"Mum . . . it's *them*," he said in an awed voice. "They're back, but they're the wrong size. They're too *wee*."

The tiny shapes waved and squeaked.

"Let me deal with this," said Signora Strega-Borgia, producing a wand from her pocket. "I'll soon have them back to life-sized." She began to mutter under her breath in Latin, passing her wand in careful circles and loops over the heads of her miniaturized family. The tiny shapes grew bigger and bigger.

"Um . . . Mum, something's gone wrong," said Titus in alarm. "Remember what you were saying about mistakes?"

The tiny shapes were now life-sized. Behind Titus, Mrs. McLachlan buried her head in her hands. Signora Strega-Borgia's face turned an unhealthy shade of gray.

"Oh, *Pandora*," said Titus sadly.

"*What?*" she yelled. "What *now*?" She followed Titus's gaze downward to where her feet should have been. "Aaaargh! What are *those*?"

"Legs," said Titus helpfully. "Eight of them."

"Oh NO," wailed Pandora. "Look at *Dad*!"

"What's wrong with me?" said Signor Strega-Borgia.

"Shall I tell him, or will you?" said Titus to his sister.

"Darling," breathed Signora Strega-Borgia, "your bottom half appears to have been confused with that of our littlest daughter. . . ."

"My bottom half . . . ," Signor Strega-Borgia repeated, looking down. "Oh yeuuchh, excuse *me*, I need a diaper change."

"And Dad, um . . . while you're about it," said Titus, blushing deep crimson, "you're wearing lipstick. . . ."

"Somehow, I don't think I'm exactly cutting a dashing figure, what with a soggy bum and fuchsia-pink lips. . . ."

"I don't care what you're wearing," said Signora Strega-Borgia loyally. "I'm just so glad to have you home."

"Oh, *baby*," cooed Mrs. McLachlan. "My little . . . *no*, my *large* Damp . . . come to Nanny, pet."

Blissfully unaware that she'd been transformed into an adult-sized infant, Damp stopped in mid-whimper and crawled toward her beloved nanny.

"Poor wee mite," said Mrs. McLachlan irrelevantly. "Let's see if we can find you something to eat."

"Better make that an adult portion," suggested Titus as the huge baby crawled slowly across the room.

"What about meEEEEE?" moaned Tarantella, crashing to the floor with a squawk. "How you bipeds manage with only two legs, I cannot imagine."

"Those are *my* legs," said Pandora, in a voice that indicated they were only out on a temporary loan.

"And all eight of those fine furry ones that you're wearing are *mine*."

"I'd better see if I can find some spells in one of my textbooks to undo this muddle," said Signora Strega-Borgia.

"Later," said her husband, wrapping his arms around her and their two older children. "Magic can wait. Right now, we have all the magic we need. . . ."

Amen to *that*, Mrs. McLachlan silently avowed, leading the enormous Damp through the door and closing it behind her.

Husband and wife hugged each other long and hard, squeezing tight, not ever wanting to let go. Titus found his eyes watering alarmingly.

Latch hoisted the ex-Pronto onto his shoulders and coughed tactfully. "Sir . . . modom . . . shall I put this in the attic for now? I imagine we shan't be needing it for some time?"

"I'm determined to get the hang of this," Tarantella muttered under her breath as, using the wall for support, she followed Latch out of the bedroom.

"Such an unflattering shade of pink," said Signora Strega-Borgia, tenderly wiping lipstick off her husband's mouth.

I haven't seen her look this happy for . . . oh, *ages*, thought Pandora.

"Come on," muttered Titus, pulling his sister out of the bedroom and closing the door behind him. "They don't need us right now."

"But, but . . . *I* need Mum," wailed Pandora, waving a hairy leg for emphasis. "She's the only one who can sort me out. Look, six surplus legs. . . ."

"Later," said Titus firmly, dragging her down the corridor. "Meanwhile, *we* have a few small matters to sort out."

"Like what?" Pandora's voice came from the ceiling. "Hey . . . being half spider, half human isn't all bad, you know. Look at MEEEEE."

She scuttled along the cornice and with a nimble leap, hung upside down from a chandelier. Titus refused to be impressed.

"Like what happened to our wager?" he insisted. "Remember? Tock? The ratlets?"

Pandora abruptly let herself down to the floor on a rope of spider silk. "Suddenly," she said, "I've got an overwhelming desire for a nice crunchy bluebottle . . . or a sun-dried daddy longlegs."

"Stop trying to change the subject."

"Titus, I can't swim the moat right now, can I? Think about it. Spiders *hate* water. All that Itsy-Bitsy up the waterspout is nonsense. Show me a swimming spider and I'll show you a little bedraggled ball of ex-arachnid."

"Absolutely," agreed Tarantella, dropping into the conversation from the floor above. "What are we talking about? Remind me—why does she have to swim the moat?"

Titus shuddered. As if his transformed sister wasn't bad enough, here was that revolting tarantula again. He took a deep breath and began, "We had a bet. She had five days to find Multitudina's babies, or else she had to swim one lap of the moat."

"*Them*," spat Tarantella, "those vile rodentettes? Those squeaky pink nastinesses? Well . . . that's *easy*. She has found them."

"She *has*?" said Titus.

"I have?" said Pandora.

"You *have*," Tarantella said firmly. "Think back. While we were enjoying the delights of exceeding the speed limit on the Web, we had a near collision. D'you recall? Coming toward us? Faster than a sneeze? Speed of light and all that stuff?"

Pandora's eyes grew wide. "Oh, that was *them*. I wondered why they seemed so familiar. . . ."

Tarantella dangled from the ceiling, her twin legs tightly folded round her body. "So let's have no more talk of moats"— she shivered—"or spiders in baths"—she shuddered—"and especially not that verminous baggage and her unspeakable off-spring."

"So I *did* find them," said Pandora wonderingly. She felt . . . oh, light, airy. Her body appeared to be filling up with millions of tiny bubbles. No bet, no moat, no CROCODILE! She extruded several feet of spider silk and launched herself off the banister into the lofty heights of the stairwell. "FREEEEEEeeeeee!" she yelled as she vanished from sight.

Tarantella sighed. Still such a drama queen. Noise and theatrics. And, she decided, the girl has a lot to learn about spinning silk. She gazed at Titus. His mouth opened and shut and opened again.

"All I want to know is what happened to them? Where did they go?"

"I neither know, nor do I care," said the spider. "And now, if you'll excuse me, I'm going home." Lurching inexpertly on her two new legs, Tarantella headed for her attic.

A Simple Twist of Fate

*P*rofessore Flense-Filleto removed his surgeon's gloves with an audible snap and dropped them in a garbage can. Over the green surgical mask, his eyes were red-rimmed with exhaustion. The operation had not been a success. In fact, due to a computer failure, it had been a disaster.

On the other side of the recovery room, the anesthesiologist frowned at his equipment and tapped it with a rubber-gloved finger. "Useless machine," he muttered, giving it a good kick. The heart monitor sprang to life, disgorging one hundred feet of graph paper from its chittering innards. "That's better," said the anesthesiologist, scanning the printout. He patted a ban-daged form lying on a gurney nearby. "Thought you'd *died* on me for a minute. . . ."

The nurse looked up from where she was counting blood-smeared scalpels onto a tray. "When he wakes up, he'll probably wish he had."

The professore groaned and massaged the bridge of his nose. "Thanks for the vote of confidence, nurse."

The hospital orderly stopped disinfecting the floor and languidly rinsed his mop in a rusted steel bucket. Pink-tinged water slopped out over its side. "What a *massacre*," he moaned, "blood everywhere . . . d'you have to be so sloppy? This job's taking me twice as long as usual, and I'm still not done yet. . . ."

"All right, ALL RIGHT!" yelled the professore. "*So.* I make a mistake, huh? We all make mistakes. Nobody is perfect. My father—rest his soul—always said to me as he filleted the pork bellies and the lamb shanks and the ox hearts, in this life, sonny, nobody's perfect . . . not even your mama."

"Hey, come on," said the anesthesiologist, "lighten up. It's hardly your fault, Professore. So there was a major fault with the computer linkup, right?" Despite the silence that greeted this question, he warmed to his theme. "So there's a bunch of nomadic rodents on the Net, right? And they get mixed up in the computer-generated model we're working from to remodel this guy's face, right? Not your fault. So this guy wakes up, right?" He prodded the silent body on the gurney. "He looks in the mirror and he goes, 'WHAT'S *THIS*?' and he sues you, right? You sue the computer company, right? The computer company sues its supplier of microprocessors—"

"Right?" interrupted the professore, catching on at last.

"The supplier of microprocessors fires a worker on its assembly line." The anesthesiologist paused for effect.

"RIGHT!" chorused the nurse and the orderly.

"And . . . ," the anesthesiologist added, "the worker on the assembly line goes home and yells at the wife and kids . . ."

"He's coming round," warned the nurse.

Don di S'Embowelli Borgia was swimming in a blood-filled fish tank. Suspended, drifting in claustrophobic redness around him were the skeletons of the hapless Ragu plus countless other bodies whose lives the Don had taken. He thrashed and gargled, trying to reach the surface . . . the light . . . the air. . . . Squeaking pitifully, he exploded into daylight . . . into an echoing steel nightmare with his senses magnified a hundredfold. The smell of disinfectant burned his bandaged nose, the light seared his bandaged eyes, and every noise crashed and boomed like thunder in his ears.

Nearby came an oceanic splashing followed by a rhythmic swish swish, then a voice grated in his ear, "If I was you, signor, I'd sue them for everything. . . ."

"Squeak, eek, squee?" said the Don.

"Feeling better, signor?" This new voice was accompanied by a deluge of cheap perfume. "Don't try to say anything just yet."

"Squeee! SQUEAK, EEE, *eek*!" said the Don.

"Bad luck, old chap," said a third voice, growing painfully loud as its owner approached where the Don lay. "We ran into some little problems during your operation, but nothing that we can't sort out with two years of intensive corrective surgery. . . ."

"Eek, EEEK SQUEEE," shrieked the Don, thrashing his bandaged head from side to side.

"NURSE!" yelled the anesthesiologist. "Hold his head, I'm going to put him under again."

The Don's plaintive squeakings grew fainter as he slipped back underneath the red tide again, his new whiskers streaming behind him. Swimming, he decided, was easier when you used your pink tail as a rudder.

Sorted

11 "Right," said Signora Strega-Borgia, with a confidence that she didn't feel. "Let's get this muddle sorted out."

The family was gathered in the library at StregaSchloss, smiling for the camera as Pandora took a photograph of them all. "Just one last one, Mum, but with me in it," she said, passing the camera to her mother and scuttling across the floor and up the wall to dangle upside down from the cornice.

Tarantella crossed and recrossed her human legs and rolled her eyes. "Oh, come *on*," she demanded peevishly, "I was halfway through the most *delicious* dinner when you dragged me back down here."

"SMILE," said Signora Strega-Borgia. They smiled and the camera captured the moment forever: Signor Strega-Borgia standing, one arm on the mantelpiece, clad in a dry diaper; Tarantella gazing into the camera, with her legs draped over the arm of a chair; Damp asleep, propped up against a pinnacle of books; Titus in his pajamas, affecting total boredom as Pandora swung back and forth in front of him, suspended on a lumpy length of spider silk. . . .

Did it flash? wondered Signora Strega-Borgia to herself, peering into the lens of the camera, before laying it down on a nearby chair.

The mantelpiece clock began to chime midnight.

"Now . . . um, let's see if I can understand this." Signora Strega-Borgia leafed through an enormous leather-bound book, chewing the end of her wand thoughtfully.

The family waited. Impatiently, Signor Strega-Borgia demanded, "Darling, are you *sure* you're going to get it right this time? What if you turn us all into cockroaches or worse?"

Signora Strega-Borgia threw her wand to the floor and burst into tears.

The library door opened to reveal Mrs. McLachlan bearing a laden tray. "Now, dear," she said, ignoring the loud sobs coming from her employer, "what we all need is a good strong cup of tea and maybe a wee fruit scone, or perhaps some of my seed cake, or fudge cake, or lemon drench cake, or plum cake, or banana loaf, or maybe," she paused, ascertained that the Signora was still weeping, ". . . or maybe you're not hungry?"

She placed the tea tray firmly on top of the open book of spells and picked up the discarded wand. "Such a nuisance, these things," she declared. "Simply not up to the job." Signora Strega-Borgia looked up, her tear-stained face showing a faint glimmer of hope. "Now, dear," continued Mrs. McLachlan, cutting the fudge cake into several generous wedges, "I've washed and ironed your best wand, and it's waiting for you on the kitchen table. Why don't you pop downstairs and get it, and meanwhile I'll pour you a cup of tea?"

Obediently, Signora Strega-Borgia headed downstairs to the kitchen. As soon as the sound of her footsteps faded away, Mrs. McLachlan pulled a small case from her pocket and fixed the family with a basilisk-like glare. "Not one *word*," she commanded, holding up her hand for silence. "Not one word now, and not a squeak when the Signora returns, or there'll be no cake. One day the Signora might become a very fine witch, but she'll never do it unless she *thinks* she can." Flipping open her case, Mrs. McLachlan began to type.

Mrs. McLachlan met Signora Strega-Borgia clutching her laundered wand in the corridor outside the library. "Not that I know the first thing about magic, dear, but . . . might I make a wee suggestion?" Signora Strega-Borgia bit her bottom lip and nodded. "I've turned out the lights in the library to aid your concentration. There's just enough light coming from the fireplace to allow you to see where to point your nice clean wand. Maybe you were just distracted last time by the sight of your loved ones in such a pickle? So . . . my advice, for what it's worth, is do *not* turn the lights back on until you're finished. That way, you won't be able to see their wee faces, and you'll be able to concentrate on doing your magic." Patting Signora Strega-Borgia on the arm, Mrs. McLachlan opened the library door and led her employer inside.

In the flickering firelight, Signora Strega-Borgia could just about make out the shapes of her family huddled by the fireplace. A thin and hairy leg waved encouragingly in her direction, followed by a hissed, "Tarantella . . . PAN, I mean, don't distract her!"

A stifled sob from Damp firmed up Signora Strega-Borgia's resolve. I *won't* fail, she decided, I simply *can't*. My family needs me. I CAN do this. I think I am a good enough witch. She amended the last bit, I AM a good enough witch. I am. I am. Slowly, holding her breath, fingers tightly crossed, she began to spin. Behind her, holding Pandora's camera, Mrs. McLachlan waited.

Just as Signora Strega-Borgia stopped in mid-spin and pointed her trembling wand at her family, Mrs. McLachlan pressed the shutter release on the camera. It flashed; Signora Strega-Borgia gasped and rushed to turn on the lights.

"Oh, well *done,* dear," said Mrs. McLachlan, prompting the family with a glare.

"Um . . . er . . . well DONE, Mum," said Titus, catching on.

"What a star," added Tarantella, clapping all eight legs.

"How ever *did* you do that?" said Signor Strega-Borgia and Pandora in perfect stereo.

"Oh . . . ," said Signora Strega-Borgia, casually stirring her teacup with her wand, "it was easy."

At least, noted Mrs. McLachlan, carrying Damp upstairs to bed, she had the grace to blush. . . .

The Taste of Summer

"Oh, Marie, you shouldn't have!" cried Mrs. McLachlan. "A cake! For my birthday! How *kind*." She hugged the blushing cook and gazed at the cake in disbelief.

"What an *unusual* color," murmured Signora Strega-Borgia. "I've always thought gray so stylish. . . . come on, Ffup, do the candles, pet."

The dragon obligingly leaned forward and squirted flames from each nostril. Immediately the entire cake was alight.

"*Fifty* candles," whispered Titus. "Eughh. I don't ever want to be *that* old."

"That can be arranged," Pandora replied.

Mrs. McLachlan took a huge breath.

"Make a wish, make a wish," Pandora pleaded.

Mrs. McLachlan winked, and exhaled.

"Bravo!" cheered Signor Strega-Borgia, lifting his glass to her. "Now your wish will come true."

"But you *can't* tell us what it was," Pandora said hopefully.

"But you *can* cut the cake," said Signora Strega-Borgia.

Marie Bain handed Mrs. McLachlan a knife and scuttled back to the kitchen for plates.

It had been a perfect day, thought Titus. If it had been *my* birthday wish, he decided, I would have wished that every day could be just like this one. Following a morning of unbroken sunshine, they had eaten lunch in the garden and now, replete and sleepy with happiness, the family and assorted pets lounged on the lawn on blankets and deck chairs, watching the sun slide into the sea loch. Late afternoon sunshine painted StregaSchloss gold, gilded them all in its gentle light, and drove the scent of honeysuckle out into the still air.

If it had been *my* birthday wish, thought Pandora as she watched Mrs. McLachlan struggle to cut through the gray icing, I'd have wished for a different cake. . . .

A shadow fell across the tablecloth. "Nonna!" Signora Strega-Borgia struggled to her feet. "What a pleasant surprise!"

"And you thought *fifty* was old . . . ," Pandora whispered to her brother.

A very wrinkly old lady was dripping over the remains of lunch. "Someone defrosted me . . . ," she mumbled, then caught sight of the cake. "How kind . . . a cake . . . for me? Is it my birthday? Again?"

"Welcome back, Nonna." Signora Strega-Borgia led the old woman to a deck chair and gently folded her into it. "Some tea? Champagne? Strawberries?"

"Have they found it yet?" the old woman asked. Her voice sounded painfully dry, like the rustle of papery leaves, words made of dust. "The *cure*, you know," she added. "You *do* remember, don't you?" Her watery eyes fixed pleadingly on Signora Strega-Borgia.

"No, Nonna," she said. "Not yet."

Strega-Nonna shrank into her deck chair. In the sunshine, her skin was almost transparent. At her feet, Sab slumped with a small grunt. The old lady smiled, causing her face to crease up like a walnut. Creaking slightly, she bent forward to pat the griffin's leathery head. "Dear faithful beast," she murmured, "you're wearing your six hundred years better than I am. . . ." The griffin looked up at her in adoration. "I miss our conversations," she mused, "our long walks. . . . That freezer is pretty lonely, I can tell you. Still . . . one day. . . ."

Two large tears squeezed out from under the griffin's eyelids.

Strega-Nonna levered herself to her feet. Painfully she bent down and took a strawberry from the fruit bowl. Titus watched, fascinated, as she popped it into her gummy mouth, mumbled it around for a moment, and swallowed. "Summer . . . ," she said, hobbling back to the house. "The taste of all those summers. . . ." She vanished into the shadowy doorway of StregaSchloss. Sab gave a small whimper.

"What did she mean, 'a cure'?" said Pandora.

"For old age, sweetheart," sniffed Signora Strega-Borgia, dabbing at her eyes with her napkin. "She's waiting till they find a cure for old age, then she'll stop living in the freezer."

"But can't you cure her?" said Titus. "You know, with a spell or something? Magic her back to being young?"

Signora Strega-Borgia sighed. "There are some things, Titus, that are way beyond my limited magical powers. A cure for old age is one of them."

The group on the lawn was silent as they considered this. A tortoiseshell butterfly alighted on the cake, sampled some of the gray icing, and keeled over with a dying beat of its wings.

"Poor Nonna," said Pandora. "It must be awful just lying there with only ice cream and fish sticks for company."

"It's her choice," said Signor Strega-Borgia. "But personally, I think she's making a big mistake. . . ."

"It's a family failing." Signora Strega-Borgia smiled at Titus. "Don't worry, she really is quite happy in her own way. Every time we have a power cut, she reappears, says hello, asks if there have been any advances in science, and then goes back to sleep. She's been doing it for *centuries*."

"What did she do before freezers were invented?" asked Titus.

"She lived near the North Pole," said his mother, "in an iceberg. Under the aurora with whales and polar bears for company, not to mention millions of cod."

"I have the plates, Meesuss McCacclong," called Marie Bain, emerging from the shadows around the house. She squinted in the sunlight, twisting her hands in her apron.

"Oh *Lord*," said Mrs. McLachlan, reminded of the cake. She renewed her efforts with the knife, but the icing remained immune to her assaults.

"What *is* this stuff?" she demanded as the knife tip snapped off and pinged into a leftover bowl of potato salad. "Concrete?"

"Yes," said the cook, blissfully unaware of the effect this admission had on the assembled company. "Ees Readymix Concrete, eet say zo on ze packet."

"Marie dear," said Mrs. McLachlan, "could you be an angel and bring me another knife? This one seems to be broken."

As the cook disappeared kitchenward once more, Mrs. McLachlan removed a small case from her pocket.

Latch sighed—There she goes again, he thought, vanity, vanity. . . .

There was a bright flash accompanied by the smell of burning sugar.

"Heavens!" Signora Strega-Borgia said admiringly, displaying an abysmal ignorance of all things culinary. "How did you do *that*? Is it like a blowtorch? A sort of portable microwave thingy? What a clever thing."

Latch stared at Mrs. McLachlan. He put two and two together and arrived at five and three quarters.

"*This* time," she said to him under her breath, "I didn't miss my target."

She raised her voice to its normal volume and added, "Marie—the knife, how very kind, dear. Now . . . cake, everyone?"

Swimming with the Crocodile

The first stars were appearing in the sky as the family finished Mrs. McLachlan's birthday lunch. The cake had been devoured down to the last smear of icing, and Knot lay under a chestnut tree, slowly chewing his way through his forty-third pink candle.

Latch and Mrs. McLachlan shook the tablecloth free of crumbs, the antique linen weave catching the last of the evening light. For an instant, they were joined by this luminous cloth as they folded and refolded it into a neat parcel.

Signor and Signora Strega-Borgia ambled down to the lochside to watch the sun leach out into the sea. Titus noted with some satisfaction that they had their arms wrapped tightly around each other.

"I think they're going to be all right, Titus," said Pandora. "We can stop worrying about them."

"Eugh, they're *kissing*," groaned Titus, his delighted expression betraying how happy he was to see his parents engaging in such revolting behavior.

Pandora sighed and rolled over onto her stomach. "I've eaten too much," she remarked happily.

"Pig," said Titus.

Pandora ignored him, reaching out to scoop leftover chicken legs and salami sandwiches into a bowl.

Titus watched her with horror. "You're not . . . ," he said.

"Eat this lot?" She balanced the bowl on top of a tureen full of potato salad. "Don't be ridiculous, I'm going to feed Tock. Keep me company?"

"I'll come in a minute." Titus yawned and stretched crabwise in the dewy grass. He watched his sister disappear round the side of StregaSchloss, heading for the moat. After a whole day of sun and food he felt too full to move just yet. Overhead, the familiar constellations winked into being, pinpricked against a lilac sky. Bats flew out from the eaves of the house, skillfully avoiding the treetops in their nocturnal quest for food.

The water in the moat was still, mirroring the moon rising over the distant hills. Pandora placed her offerings on the warm stone that rimmed Tock's home, and sat down to wait. On the far bank, a frantic thrashing amongst the water lilies indicated that she wouldn't have to linger long.

With a series of rusty creaks and honks, Tock's snout broke water three feet away from Pandora. Ancient yellow eyes met her green ones. Pandora shivered. The sight of all those teeth, askew like tombstones in a disused graveyard, reminded her of her recent narrow escape. Tock's nostrils flared as he caught wind of his dinner. He sped toward it, throwing up a wave in his wake. Pandora leapt to her feet and jumped backward, just as the crocodile hurled itself out of the water.

Much to Pandora's relief, she was not the reason for Tock's haste. The crocodile ignored her completely, burying his nose in the pile of salami sandwiches. Greedily he opened his jaws wide and then appeared to undergo a change of heart. After devouring two of Pronto's henchmen plus their knife and machine gun, the crocodile had taken a vow never to touch flesh again, especially not of the weapon-bearing kind.

"Blark," he honked, pointing to the salami. "Glurk ploot phitui."

"I beg your pardon?" Pandora said, not understanding one word.

"Glop. Splug . . . drekk," explained Tock, de-salami-ing the sandwiches and tossing the discarded pink circles into the undergrowth.

"You don't like salami?" Pandora inquired.

"Drekk yrrg. Meat-blah," Tock said, investigating the contents of the tureen.

"You're a recent convert to vegetarianism?" Pandora said, astonished. In her mind, a wild plan began to take shape.

"Gaw titin wun," Tock said, wolfing potato salad. On reflection, he picked up the tureen and ate it as well. Displaying alarming amounts of teeth in a grin, he waddled back into the moat and glided effortlessly away into the darkness just as Titus came looking for his sister.

To Titus's horror, he arrived in time to see Pandora strip down to her underwear and dip a foot in the water of the moat. She's *not*, he thought, breaking into a run.

Without turning her head to show that she'd spotted him,

Pandora said, "So. I'm a wuss, am I? A scaredy sissy? A cowardy cuss?"

"Pan. Don't do it. The bet's off."

"Maybe so," she said, straightening her arms out in front of her, "but you'll always think that I ratted on the deal."

"No. Well . . . maybe," admitted Titus.

Pandora rose on her toes and brought her arms together over her head. On the far side of the moat, in an area of deepest shade, something stirred. Something that hadn't eaten a nanny for weeks.

"Please, Pandora—DON'T DO THIS," Titus begged, reaching the moatside at exactly the same time as his sister dived into the water. Large waves splashed over the stone surround, soaking Titus's feet. From the area of deepest darkness, a wave of displaced water arrowed toward Pandora's point of entry. "OH NO. . . ." Titus was terrified.

This was worse than sending your baby sibling down the Internet, far worse than finding your mother drunk, worse even than being held at gunpoint. . . . He simply couldn't imagine life without Pandora. As he flung himself into the moat, Titus remembered that for him, swimming lessons had been a complete washout. WHAT AM I DOING? He panicked, water closing over his head. I CAN'T EVEN SWIM AND THERE'S A RAVENING REPTILE IN HERE SOMEWHERE. . . .

"HELP!" he screamed, surfacing. "HELP! HELP! I'M DROWNING!"

"Don't be such a wuss," said a familiar voice.

I'm dead, thought Titus, I'm hearing things. An unstoppable force propelled him at full speed across the moat. Titus opened his eyes. He was pinioned across Tock's snout. "NO!" he shrieked. "HELP! I'M BEING EATEN BY A CROCODILE! SAVE ME!"

In exasperation the crocodile's slitty eyes rolled backward in its head. With an effortless jerk of his neck muscles, Tock tossed Titus onto his scaly back and set off across the moat again.

Suddenly remembering why he'd jumped into the moat in the first place, Titus wrapped his arms around Tock's neck and tried to throttle his sister's assassin.

"Aaah," said Tock. No one had ever hugged him before. To show his appreciation, he playfully nibbled Titus's arms.

"AAUGHH. HE'S GOT ME! I'M DYING!"

"Titus, for heaven's sake, do shut up."

"Pandora? You're *alive*?"

"Yes. And so are you," Pandora said, treading water in front of him. "Tock, let *go* of him."

The crocodile released his grip on Titus's arms.

To Titus's embarrassment, they weren't even scratched.

"Titus, what are you doing in the moat?"

"Rescuing you from this beast."

"Oh, Titus . . . what a *brave* thing to do."

"No," Titus said, edging warily along Tock's back, away from the rows of teeth, "it wasn't brave, it was stu—"

His words were lost in an explosion of bubbles as Tock dived underwater. Titus found himself gripped in a strong pair of arms and towed back to the surface again.

"Pandora," he spluttered, half-drowned. "What are you doing?"

"Rescuing *you*, brother mine." She expertly struck out for dry land, cupping Titus's chin in her hand. "Rescuing you from yourself. . . ."

"Why didn't you tell me?" Latch moaned. "Instead of letting me make an idiot of myself. . . ."

Mrs. McLachlan gazed up at the night sky where the wheeling shapes of Sab and Ffup were silhouetted against the stars. "You didn't make an idiot of yourself, dear. On the contrary, you were exceedingly brave."

"But that case of yours," insisted Latch. "You should have said . . ."

Mrs. McLachlan dropped her gaze to meet his. "Said *what?*" she demanded. "'Oh, Latch, here I have a wee case that combines a superintelligent computer with some good old-fashioned magic, so step back and let little old me take care of this gun-wielding criminal. . . .' or, 'Move over, dear, and let a real witch take care of this.' Get real, laddie—you'd never have believed me."

"Um"—Latch scratched furiously under his kilt—"er . . . yes . . . you're absolutely right. But I believe you *now.*" He paused and suddenly pleaded, "Flora—could you use it, the case, to do something about this stupid tartan skirt?"

Mrs. McLachlan's laughter rang out over the meadow, merging with the distant putter of the nighttime lobster boat that tracked a line of silver across the sea loch.

In the Schloss kitchen, Marie Bain dozed in an ancient settle, her slipperless feet propped on Knot's woolly back, a cookbook open spine up across her lap.

In the cellar, the mended freezer hummed and clicked, drawing Strega-Nonna deeper and deeper into permafrost.

"Titus," said Pandora, appearing at his bedroom door.

"Nhuh?" He looked up from the pages of a computer manual.

"Can I come in? My bedroom's a dump, I've got nothing to read, and I've only got a pile of broken matchsticks to sleep on."

"You think *you've* got problems," Titus said, flicking through his manual. "My CD-ROM's broken. I took it apart and found *some*one had stuffed bacon rinds in it."

"Yeuuchhh," said Pandora. "That sounds like the kind of stunt that Damp would pull. . . ."

"Babies are so gross," said Titus.

"I'm *never* going to have any when I'm old," said Pandora.

"I'm *never* going to grow old," vowed Titus. "*Fifty* candles!"

"Six *hundred* candles," groaned Pandora.

"You'd never be able to blow them out," said Titus.

"Fancy a little wager?" said Pandora.

"*NO,*" said Titus.

Damp stretched like a small starfish. Her parents on either side of her groaned and clung on to their tiny allowance of edge-of-bed. The baby lay in the darkness, surrounded by the smell of sleep that clung to the comforter, debating whether to whimper, grizzle, or go back to sleep. Something had woken her up. Her eyes flicked open. There it was again—a scratching noise. She couldn't see anything, even with the full moon shining across the bedroom and pooling on the floor over by the fireplace. Damp's eyelids closed slowly, her eyelashes casting long shadows across her cheeks. Her mothlike breath changed to something heavier, and within moments, she was deeply asleep.

Under the bed, Multitudina groaned and clutched her distended stomach with both front paws. Never, never, never again, she vowed. Too much like hard work, she reminded herself in between groans. And besides, she thought frivolously, I'll *never* get my girlish figure back if I keep on having babies. Two minutes later, she was gazing in surprise at a tiny pink replica of herself. Was that it? she wondered, just the *one*? Phew, got off lightly, then—here was me expecting to be expecting at least six. . . . The tiny bald ratlet opened its mouth to demand room service. As for your name, Multitudina thought, expertly tucking her daughter under one arm, I've decided to call you Terminus. . . .

A Word from Debi Gliori

The title *Pure Dead Magic* harks back to my teenagehood in Glasgow. It was the phrase we employed to reassure, flatter, and smooth ruffled feathers, as in:

"Don't I look like a fat blob in these trousers?"

"Naww, you look pure dead magic."

As you can see, it means "very fine indeed, verging on the excellent." Pure dead *anything* is a Glaswegian way of underlining your point. As in: "How was school today, darling?" Now, you might say, "It was very boring, but thank you for asking." Glaswegians would say, "Och, it was pure dead boring."

As to pronunciation, you really need the authentic Glaswegian twang to do it justice. To achieve the requisite gravel-throated growliness, you might want to eat fifty-five crackers in a row, thus rendering your mouth as arid as the Gobi Desert. Now pinch your nose closed between forefinger and thumb and try to say the title the way Sean Connery would when he said, "Namesh Bond, Jamesh Bond." Urrr. Rrrrrghhh. Ochhh.

Perfect. Pure dead magic, in fact. We'll make an honorary Scot of you yet.

Don't miss the new adventures of the
Strega-Borgia clan in

PURE
DEAD
WICKED!

For a sneak peek, turn the page. . . .

Elementary Magic

Much later, Titus was to remark that this must have been the only time in history when a dirty diaper could be said to have saved several lives.

On that memorable morning, unaware of the terrible danger that hung over their heads, the Strega-Borgia family had been attempting to squash themselves into the interior of their long-suffering family car. Their shopping trip to the nearby village of Auchenlochtermuchty was long overdue, and consequently, all members of the family of two adults and three children were vociferous in their demands that they should not be left behind at home. Titus needed a computer magazine, Pandora had to buy something to eradicate a minuscule crop of pimples that had erupted on her chin, their baby sister, Damp, required more diapers, and their parents, Signor and Signora Strega-Borgia, had to go to the bank and do boring adult stuff.

As was usual with any planned expedition between

StregaSchloss and Auchenlochtermuchty, the process of leaving the house was taking longer than anticipated. Boots and coats had to be retrieved from the cloakroom, Damp had to be supplied with a clean diaper and given a ration of crackers to stave off starvation, and Titus needed to render himself deaf to everything going on around him by the simple expedient of clamping a pair of headphones round his head and pressing the ON button on his Walkman.

Titus threw himself into the car seat next to Damp, turned up the volume, and settled back with a smile. From outside the car, where she stood with her parents as they went through the ritual of finding checkbooks and car keys, Pandora noted with some satisfaction that Titus's expression was changing rapidly to one of disgust.

"PHWOARRR!" he bawled, competing with the deafening sounds inside his headphones. "DAMP! THAT'S DISGUST-ING!"

He struggled with his seat belt, desperate to put as much distance as possible between himself and Damp's odious diaper. Signor Strega-Borgia groaned, unbuckling his baby daughter and plucking her out of her car seat. Just at the precise moment that both Damp and Titus exited the car, the unthinkable happened.

A trio of vast and ancient roof slates that had clung to the topmost turret of StregaSchloss for six hundred years, held in place by little more than a clump of moss, broke free of their moorings and began their downward descent. Gathering momentum by the second, they barreled down the steep incline of the roof.

It all happened so quickly that initially the family were convinced that, for reasons unknown, an invisible bomber had dropped its payload directly onto their car. One minute they were standing around the unfortunate vehicle, happily slandering Damp's diaper, the next they were lying groaning on the rose-quartz drive, wondering what had hit them.

"What on earth?" Signor Strega-Borgia picked himself and Damp off the ground and ran to Signora Strega-Borgia to check that she was unharmed.

"Titus? Pan? Are you all right? Whatever happened?" Signora Strega-Borgia rubbed dirt off her clothes and stared at the car in disbelief.

"WHAT A WRECK!" yelled Titus, still muffled in his headphones. "LOOK AT IT! IT'S TOTALLY TRASH—*OWW!*"

"There," said Pandora with satisfaction. "That should help."

"Did you *have* to do that?" moaned Titus, holding his ears and glaring at his sister. His headphones dangled from Pandora's hands.

Signor Strega-Borgia was walking slowly round the wreckage of his car, surveying it from various angles, simultaneously horrified at the damage and amazed at the family's lucky escape. Embedded in the roof of the car, at a forty-five-degree angle to the battered paintwork, were three huge slabs of slate.

"We could all have been killed," said Signor Strega-Borgia reproachfully. He squinted up at the turreted roof of StregaSchloss, attempting to locate the origin of this attempt on his life. Beside him, Signora Strega-Borgia sighed. This was proving to be the most expensive morning's shopping thus far. To their list of items to be purchased in Auchenlochtermuchty, they now had to add one roof and one family car.

"We'll have to get it fixed," decided Signor Strega-Borgia.

"The whole roof looks like it's in danger of raining down on top of our heads."

The family automatically took several hasty steps backward, away from the danger zone. Titus tripped over a low stone wall and fell backward into a herbaceous border with a dismayed howl. Ignoring her son completely, Signora Strega-Borgia addressed her husband. "But that will cost a *fortune*, Luciano. Look, before we call in the experts, why don't you let me see if I can mend it. I'm sure there was something I learnt at college that would do the trick."

"Darling, I hardly think that your diploma in Primary Magic is a sufficient qualif—" He halted abruptly, alerted by the glacial expression crossing his wife's face.

Throwing her black pashmina dramatically across her shoulders, Signora Strega-Borgia stalked away from her husband across the rose quartz until she stood at the head of the steps leading down to the old croquet lawn. "I know you think I'm a half-baked witch, incapable, incompetent . . ."—she choked back a sob—". . . inconsequential."

The front door opened and Mrs. Flora McLachlan, nanny to Titus, Pandora, and Damp, emerged into the December chill, shivering as she surveyed the family and their ex-car. "Now, dear," she admonished, gazing fondly at Signora Strega-Borgia, "there's no need to be like that. We all know that you're a very fine witch, indeed. . . ."

"Do we?" muttered Pandora.

"I don't *think* so," whispered Titus, crawling out of the herbaceous border and coming to stand next to his sister. Beside them, Signor Strega-Borgia sighed. If only Baci wasn't so *prickly*. He hadn't meant to insult her. Not really. Just perhaps to remind her that six months into a seven-year degree course in Advanced Magic might mean that her skills weren't exactly up to speed—yet.

"I'll prove you wrong," Signora Strega-Borgia promised, thrusting her arms wide apart and throwing back her head. Unfortunately this had the effect of making her look like a demented bat, and Titus had to avert his gaze to avoid bursting out laughing.

"My dear," said Mrs. McLachlan in alarm, "remember, if you would, that anger can cloud your judgment. Now let's not be too hasty. . . ." The nanny started down the steps toward her employer, but it was too late. Signora Strega-Borgia had already produced a small Disposawand from her handbag and was waving it erratically in front of her face.

"Healerum, Holerum . . . ," she began.

"Oh, no," sighed Pandora, "not *that* one."

"Stick . . ." Signora Strega-Borgia paused, racked her brain for the correct sequence of words, and continued undeterred, "Stickitum Quickitum, Renderum Fix."

There was a flash, a small apologetic puff of pink smoke, and the air was filled with the inappropriate smell of antiseptic cream.

"Oh, *dear*!" wailed Signora Strega-Borgia, covering her face with her hands.

"Oh, dear is right," groaned Titus.

"Oh, for heaven's sake, Baci. Just *don't* attempt to fix the car." Signor Strega-Borgia strode across the drive with Damp under one arm, stamped up the stairs into the house, and, seconds later, they all heard the sound of the bathroom door slamming shut.

Mrs. McLachlan, her mouth twitching with suppressed laughter, came over to where Signora Strega-Borgia stood hunched under her shawl, shoulders shaking, little sobs escaping from between her fingers.

"Och, pet," the nanny soothed, "it's not the end of the world. There's rain forecast for this afternoon, and that'll wash it off, and then we can call in a firm to mend the roof in a more . . . um . . . traditional fashion."

Signora Strega-Borgia peered out from between her fingers. "Oh, Flora," she wailed, "I'm useless. I mean, look at it. Look at what I've done."

At this moment, the sun chose to slide out from behind the clouds and spotlight the vast Band-Aid stuck to the topmost turret of StregaSchloss. The vision of eight hundred and sixty square feet of pink perforated plastic set against the gray slates of the roof was a little disquieting. With a wail, Signora Strega-Borgia ran for the house, her black shawl flapping behind in her wake.

"Oh, poor Mum," said Titus, horribly embarrassed by the sight of female tears. "I'd better go and see if I can cheer her up." He ran after his mother, leaving Pandora and Mrs. McLachlan gazing up at the bandaged roof.

"Can't *you* fix it?" said Pandora. "You know, with your amazing magic makeup case thing?"

The nanny immediately put her finger to her lips and made a shushing sound.

Pandora frowned and persisted. "Remember? Last summer?

You had that . . . that sort of transformer that changed . . ." She faltered. Mrs. McLachlan's expression was not even remotely encouraging. Moreover, the nanny's eyes had stopped twinkling. Pandora shivered. Suddenly she felt chilled to the bone.

"Heavens, is that the time?" Mrs. McLachlan gazed at her watch. "My fudge cake will be ready to come out of the oven in one minute. And you, young lady—not only are you appallingly inquisitive, you're also freezing cold. Come, child, inside with you." Taking Pandora's arm, she propelled her in the direction of the house. On the doorstep she paused and placed a gentle finger on Pandora's lips. "One: I can't fix the roof. Two: I don't have the makeup case anymore. Three: I swapped it for something better, and . . ."

"Four?" said Pandora hopefully.

"If I promise to tell you more when the time is right, would you please forget that we ever had this conversation?"

"Yes, I promise," said Pandora, bursting with unanswered questions, "but—"

"No buts," said Mrs. McLachlan in such a way as to indicate that not only was the subject closed, it was bolted, padlocked, and, in all probability, nailed shut.

With a thwarted snort, Pandora followed Mrs. McLachlan inside.

The Money Hum

From as far back as anyone could remember, there had always been somebody mending the roof at StregaSchloss. A succession of roofers with good heads for heights had clambered over its slates, scaled its pointy turrets, and once, memorably, poured hot lead over a particularly leaky section. This had caused the attic to burst into flames and initiated a temporary diaspora of several thousand attic-dwelling spiders.

Like the Forth Road Bridge, the roof at StregaSchloss was never finished. No sooner had one tribe of tradesmen vanished into the surrounding hills clutching a large check than another would appear, bearing scaffolding and slates, a stack of small newspapers with large headlines, and several tartan thermos flasks. Two days after the incident with the slipping slates, the Strega-Borgias braced themselves for the arrival of yet another firm of roofing contractors.

There was a pattern to this, Titus observed, stepping around a brimming soup tureen placed strategically under a leak from the cupola of the great hall. First of all, the roofers would arrive and consult with Mum. There would be much sucking in of air through teeth (the ferocity of the inhalation indicating how expensive the work was going to be). This would be followed by the traumatic discovery that none of their cell phones would work this far into the wilds of Argyll. Next came the erection of a web of rusty scaffolding; this was Titus's favorite stage, since his vocabulary of spectacular Anglo-Saxon curses had been garnered entirely from listening to these roofing tribes at work.

Titus practiced a few of these as his bare toes made contact with a particularly squelchy bit of rug in the great hall.

"I *heard* that," muttered Mrs. McLachlan, who came striding along the corridor from the kitchen. "I've lost Damp again," she said, "and I did hear the postman, but where's the post gone?"

A distant flushing sound followed by a cacophony of StregaSchloss plumbing alerted them both to Damp's whereabouts.

"FOR HEAVEN'S SAKE!" yelled Mrs. McLachlan. "DAMP! STOP IT!" And she shot along the corridor, expertly hurdling over brimming bowls and buckets in a futile attempt to divert the baby from her discovery that flush toilets can make all sorts of things disappear.

Titus ambled into the kitchen in search of breakfast. An alien reek of powerful aftershave assailed his nostrils. The source of this proved to be a balding man sprawled over the kitchen table across from Signora Strega-Borgia. Papers and glossy brochures were spread out amongst coffee cups and breakfast detritus. Titus's mother was frowning as she scribbled numbers on the back of an envelope.

Boring, thought Titus, scanning the shelves in the fridge. Yeuch, he amended, discovering a promising paper bag to be full of yellowing Brussels sprouts.

"Look at it this way, Mrs. Sega-Porsche," said the balding man, waving his coffee cup expansively. "It's like your dentist telling you that your teeth are fine but your gums have to come out. . . ."

"I'm not exactly sure that I understand," muttered Signora Strega-Borgia, frowning even more deeply and looking up from her envelope.

"Your coffee's wonderful, by the way," said Baldy, taking a slurp for emphasis, "best I've had for ages. . . . Anyway, your roof's fine. Great. Tip-top. Fantastic."

"And?" sighed Signora Strega-Borgia.

Titus found what he was looking for and slipped it into his pajama pocket.

"Excuse me, Mr. Pile-Um," said Signora Strega-Borgia.

"Pylum-Haight," interjected the bald man.

"*Indeed.*" Signora Strega-Borgia's voice developed a marked windchill factor.

"Excuse me. Titus, put that back."

"Mu-ummm, just a wee drop."

"Put it *back*, Titus. I'm in no mood for an argument."

"But I want to see if it works," pleaded Titus, adding somewhat cuttingly, "None of your other spells ever do. . . ."

Signora Strega-Borgia stood up, sending brochures cascading to the kitchen floor. Titus sighed and handed her a small glass vial. Signora Strega-Borgia sat down again and flashed her visitor a patently insincere smile as she placed the vial on the table in front of her.

Mr. Pylum-Haight could read the label on the side of the vial, magnified through the glass of the coffeepot.

Tincture of Flup-tooth
to be diluted x 10
5 ml equivalent to 1 Battalion

Mentally logging this knowledge under Weird Things Clients Keep in Their Fridges, Mr. Pylum-Haight pressed on. "As I was saying, your roof is in great shape, but the beams supporting it . . ."—pause to suck in dramatic lungfuls of air—"rotten to the core, m'fraid. In fact, you're really lucky the whole thing hasn't collapsed on you, what with all the rain we've been having. . . ." Meeting Signora Strega-Borgia's steely glare, he faltered and took a deep draft of chilly coffee to sustain himself.

"So . . . Mr. Pylum-Haight . . . what exactly *are* we talking about?" Signora Strega-Borgia folded her calculation-laden envelope into a small parcel and pushed it to one side.

Titus sat at the other end of the kitchen table and waited. Now, he guessed, was not the time to raise the question of an increase in pocket money in line with inflation.

"A rough estimate—ballpark figure, off the top of my head, can't be too definite about this, not set in stone, but possibly in the region of, give or take a few . . . um . . ."

"*How much?*" insisted Signora Strega-Borgia.

Pylum-Haight hastily scribbled a figure on the back of a business card and stood up. "Have a wee think," he advised. "It's a big job. Expensive business keeping on top of these old houses. I know several clients who would be willing to take it off your hands. Get yourself something more manageable. More modern. Maybe your husband might like to give me a ring to discuss..." His voice tailed off as he busied himself with folding and packing the tableful of brochures and papers back into his crocodile-skin attaché case. "Nice to...um... thanks for the...er... We'll be in touch," he muttered, sidling in the direction of the kitchen door. "See myself out...um... thanks again." And he tiptoed backward out into the corridor, leaving a trail of aftershave behind him.

Titus listened to the sound of footsteps fade into silence. The front door creaked open and, seconds later, slammed shut. Over the faint ticking of the kitchen clock came the sound of a car engine, a crunch of gravel under tires, and the valedictory honk as Tock the moat-guarding crocodile bid the parting guest farewell.

"Mum?"

"Not right now, Titus," mumbled Signora Strega-Borgia, waving a hand absently around her head, as if to ward off a fly. She gazed at the business card in front of her as if it might be coated with plague bacteria. "I need to find your dad." She reluctantly picked up the card and rose to her feet like a sleepwalker.

"He's upstairs mending my modem," said Titus. "Mum— what's the matter? I'm sorry I made that comment about your spells. I didn't mean it."

Signora Strega-Borgia turned, her face pale and drawn. "It's not your attack on my skills as a witch, Titus. No, it's nothing"—she glanced hastily at the card in her hand—"nothing that six hundred and eighty-six thousand, eight hundred and seventy-five pounds, seventy-two p plus VAT won't fix."

The kitchen door closed behind her as Titus was left staring bleakly at the tabletop in front of him. Picking up a discarded brochure and his mother's pencil, he calculated that, at his current rate of pocket money, it would take him a mere three and a half centuries to acquire that kind of sum. The brochure showed a picture of an ideal family in front of their new home. There were a dog, a cat, a baby, and two grinning children flanked by their smiling parents. The new home behind them was built on a model that a five-year-old might draw: a front door, one window on each side, three windows above, and a perfect leak-free roof on top. The blurb read: "The Buccleuch family at home in Bogginview. Homes to depend on. Homes to raise your family in. BOGGINVIEW. Another quality build from BELLAVISTA INC. . . ."

Not even remotely like *our* house, thought Titus. If they'd decided to make a brochure about StregaSchloss, we'd be scowling on the moth-eaten croquet lawn: "The Strega-Borgias at home with their dragon, their yeti, their griffin, and . . . oh, yes, their moat-guarding crocodile. Behind them, you can just see their modest little STREGASCHLOSS, which looks like a cross between a fairy castle and the film set for *Vlad the Vampire Falls on Hard Times*. . . ."

Titus threw the brochure back on the table and stalked out of the kitchen. And I just *bet* that the Buccleuch fridge is full of pizzas and chocolate fudge cake, instead of moldy Brussels sprouts, he decided, skirting an overflowing chamber pot on his way upstairs. No wonder they're grinning, he concluded.

Will young Varjak Paw survive on the Outside and save his family?

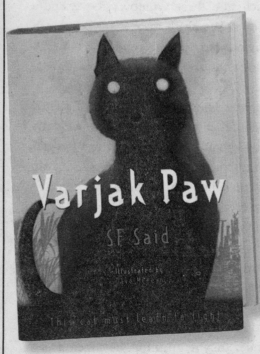

Varjak Paw is a Mesopotamian Blue kitten. He lives a sheltered life high up on a hill in an old house, until his grandfather tells him about the Way—a secret martial art for cats. In order to save his family, Varjak is forced to run away.

Now Varjak must use the Way to survive in a city full of dangerous dogs, cat gangs, and strangest of all, the mysterious Vanishings.

The classic battle of good and evil told in a whole new way!

Available May 2003!   www.randomhouse.com/kids